Freshmen

Other titles in The American Teen Writer Series:

Eighth Grade

Getting There

Juniors

Outsiders and Others

Short Takes

Something like a Hero

Sophomores

Taking Off

White Knuckles

Writing Tall

Published by Merlyn's Pen, Inc.
4 King Street
P.O. Box 1058
East Greenwich, Rhode Island 02818-0964

Printed in the United States of America.

Cover design by Alan Greco Design.
Cover illustration by Paul Olson. Copyright ©1996.

Library of Congress Cataloging-in-Publication Data

Freshmen
p. cm.
Summary: A collection of short stories on various topics, all written by American teenage writers in the ninth grade.
ISBN 1-886427-09-7
1. Short stories, American. 2. Youths' writings, American.
[1. Short stories. 2. Youths' writings.]
PZ5.F894 1997
[Fic]--dc20 96-25029
CIP
AC

99 98 97 96 6 5 4 3 2 1

Freshmen

FICTION, FANTASY, AND HUMOR
BY NINTH GRADE WRITERS

Edited by
Christine Lord

The American Teen Writer Series
Editor: R. James Stahl

Merlyn's Pen, Inc.
East Greenwich, Rhode Island

Acknowledgments

Jo-Ann Langseth, copy editor, is gratefully acknowledged for her significant work in preparing these manuscripts for original publication in *Merlyn's Pen: The National Magazines of Student Writing.*

All of the short stories and essays in this book originally appeared in *Merlyn's Pen: The National Magazines of Student Writing.*

The American Teen Writer Series

Young adult literature. What does it mean to you?

Classic titles like *Lord of the Flies* or *Of Mice and Men*—books written by adults, for adult readers, that also are studied extensively in high schools?

Books written for teenagers by adult writers admired by teens—like Gary Paulsen, Norma Klein, Paul Zindel?

Shelves and shelves of popular paperbacks about perfect, untroubled, blemish-free kids?

Titles like *I Was a Teenage Vampire*? *Lunch Hour of the Living Dead*?

The term "young adult literature" is used to describe a range of exciting literature, but it has never accounted for the stories, poetry, and nonfiction actually written by young adults. African American literature is written by African Americans. Native American stories are penned by Native Americans. The Women's Literature aisle is stocked with books by women. Where are the young adult writers in young adult literature?

Teen authors tell their own stories in *Merlyn's Pen: The National Magazines of Student Writing*. Back in 1985 the magazine began giving young writers a place for their most compelling work. Seeds were planted. Now, the American Teen Writer Series brings us the bountiful, rich fruit of their labors.

Older readers might be tempted to speak of these authors as potential writers, the great talents of tomorrow. We say: Don't. Their talent is alive and present. Their work is here and now.

About the Author Profiles:

The editors of the American Teen Writer Series have decided to reprint the author profiles as they appeared in *Merlyn's Pen* when the authors' works were first published. Our purpose is to reflect the writers' school backgrounds and interests at the time they wrote these stories.

Contents

Noitaerc.*

The End

by Atief Heermance

The man slowly maneuvered the dark blue sedan to the facade of the large gray building and stopped, allowing the car's engine to slowly shudder until it fell silent. He paused for a moment and then lethargically climbed out of the car, a brisk autumn wind drawing a few papers from his car and scattering them across the pavement. Pulling his black overcoat and wide-brimmed hat tighter, he circled over to the parking meter to the left of his car, drew out a quarter, and then stopped, hearing a distant peal of thunder. He looked skyward in time to see a brilliant flash of lightning illuminate the distant storm clouds. The man looked from the black clouds, rapidly approaching, to the quarter in his hand, and then to the rolled-down windows of his car. A flurry of movement made him turn his head in time to see two couples ducking into an obscure café to avoid the coming storm. The man let the quarter fall to the ground, its tintinnabular ring drawing the curious gaze of a young lady. He turned and began to walk up the stairs to the building's entrance, his laughter lost in the wind. A sharp crack of thunder sounded as the large oaken doors slammed shut.

25 minutes

The man walked toward a formally dressed young man stoically positioned next to two large, polished mahogany doors. The man's shoes echoed upon the tiles, the only sound within the large hallway. The young doorman glanced nervously in his direction, quickly stepped over to his platform, and opened a large, leather-bound book.

The man stepped in front of the youth and, in a soft voice, murmured, "I'm Dr. Feryl Dalen. I believe that I am supposed to be speaking tonight."

The youth looked down at his book and smiled. "Ah yes . . . They've been expecting you for some time now."

As he moved to open the door, his wrist was roughly grabbed by Dr. Dalen, who brusquely pushed him aside. "Leave," he muttered, removing his hat with a flourish.

The young man took a step back and, noticing for the first time Dr. Dalen's previously shadowed face, began to run for the exit, throwing the doors wide and leaping down the stairs. A howling tendril of the gathering storm slammed the doors shut behind him.

Dr. Dalen laughed, positioned his hat back upon his head, and opened the doors.

23 minutes

Immediately, all talking ceased within the room. The large congregation of people, most of them still finishing their desserts, immediately turned their heads toward the ominous dark figure in the doorway. Dr. Dalen closed the doors and began to slowly work his way along the side wall up to the stage, feeling the wondering gazes of the assembled scientists upon him. *Good*, he thought. *They are beginning to feel a modicum of fear. That will make this much easier, and much more enjoyable!* He climbed upon the stage and turned to face the hushed audience. Glancing through the crowd of about two hundred men and women, he began to pick out the faces of those who were the most important. *Yes*, he thought, *there is Dr. Sajadein. It is reassuring to know that even* his *usual arrogance can be dispelled under the correct circumstances.* He set down his briefcase, stepped up to the podium, and turned on the microphone. In the distance, another crack of thunder sounded.

Dr. Dalen removed his hat and smiled as a horrified gasp ran through the audience. "No more games!" he hissed through a dark red slit on his forehead. "The planet I come from does not exist in this galaxy, and the galaxy you come from will not exist in about half an hour."

19 minutes

Dr. Dalen slowly removed and folded his overcoat, flexing two leathery tentacles as the assembled scientists looked on in horrified silence. Upon the removal of his wig, a startled cry arose from the back of the hall and a rather portly man (Dr. Dalen recognized him as a prominent astronomer) fainted. Dr. Dalen removed the large x'th wyrlyn, a glossy, slug-like creature native to his planet, from the top of his head and placed it against the aperture in his neck, where it slithered easily inside.

"Ahh . . . I suppose the one time I truly feel alone is when my x'th wyrlyn is away from me. I liken it to what you humans call 'pets'. Ah well . . . I suppose the question foremost in your minds is, 'Why have I assembled you, Gaia's most prominent scientists, here tonight?' I will state it thusly. I deem you worthy to know why I have dwelled within your midst for so long. Listen, and I will explain . . . that is, until we are all killed."

Dr. Dalen paused and took a drink from a nearby glass of water, efficiently siphoning its contents into his forehead with one sharp *SSSSP!*

"As most of you are aware," he continued, "the universe has been expanding since the beginning of time. It is useless to attempt to comprehend or explain time before the universe, as all laws that we know of break down at the Big Bang, or *ferrs'hirici* as it is called in my language. At the moment of the Big Bang, the known universe was somehow compressed into an atom of near-infinite density. It is absurd to say, as some have proposed, that the universe was at infinite density, because regardless of what speed matter was released at in the resulting explosion, the atom would still remain infinite. Thus, the gravitational pull would immediately suck the matter back in. However, at the moment, the density is irrelevant. Upon reaching either state, the power locked within the atom would also become near-infinite and would immediately cause the atom to detonate. To give you an idea of the amount of energy generated one second after the Big Bang, the radiation released would have reached the temperature of 100,000 million degrees.

"The universe has continued to expand ever since, atoms swirling together to form planets and stars, with these becoming solar systems and then galaxies. This is the way of the universe, and the process continues, even now. However, a problem arises from this, a problem you humans have pondered for a very long time. As galaxies are created, more mass is added to the universe. This, in turn, increases the gravitational pull upon the universe's expanding border. No race previously had the knowledge to discern the speed at which the universe expands, but it was known that if the universe was not expanding at a speed above a critical rate, it would eventually cease its expansion and begin to recede, until it was again an atom.

"Known only to a few people within this room, there is a way to detect the expansion of the universe. My people have known of it for many Gaia years, but you humans have, with my intervention, only recently 'discovered' it. The way I speak of involves the matter known as Phytec."

Dr. Dalen paused as Dr. Sajadein, fear replaced by his usual look of quiet arrogance, slowly rose to his feet. He was a tall man, lithe and muscular, with a gray-streaked Vandyke beard and a receding hairline. He positioned his spectacles, turned, and addressed the scientists.

"I believe," he said, his soft voice carrying through the hall, "that I can clarify the matter. Phytec was discovered during our efforts to induce fusion within a laser pressure chamber. The lasers' attempt to fuse two hydrogen atoms together caused the atoms to become so dense that they literally ripped through the space-time continuum. To understand this, you must understand what the space-time continuum is like. Imagine a tablecloth stretched taut. When a metal sphere is placed upon the cloth, it will sag. If a marble is then also placed upon the cloth, it will roll toward the sphere. This, then, is what gravity is like. Every object is upon its own 'tablecloth', its density determining how low the cloth sags, thus attracting an object, or rather, causing an object to roll toward it. Phytec actually rips through the cloth. It is a hole within the fabric of the space-time continuum. The only way it can be detected is by the particles it emits in certain increments of time."

Dalen coughed, and Dr. Sajadein went silent.

"A rather crude simile, Sajadein, but an appropriate one. However, you did not finish. Those few who had been studying the Phytec noticed something peculiar in the rate of emissions. Your . . . *our* instruments began to detect the particle emissions more often. As the Phytec is outside the space-time continuum, we must be measuring the particles faster because . . . the universe itself is slowing down."

A low murmur ran through the crowd as Dr. Dalen momentarily went silent. When he spoke again, there was a sound . . . a feeling in his voice that no human could identify. "I have tampered with your measurements. You believe you still have many years before the universe stops expanding. You are wrong. In reality, you have about . . . 15 minutes."

11 minutes

A few scientists began to rise, when Dr. Dalen lifted a tentacle upward. “Do NOT leave. I must finish, and if you were going to be with a loved one, you would, assuming that person is currently more than one mile away, have on the order of three minutes before your galaxy was annihilated.” The room fell silent for a moment, and then the scientists reluctantly sat back down, leaving only Dr. Sajadein still standing.

Dr. Sajadein turned and looked at Dalen questioningly. “But . . .” he began, “our universe is not going to blow up. It, and thus time, will merely stop and then begin to reverse its motion, correct?”

Dalen smiled, a sight that caused many in the room to avert their eyes at the horrible mockery of a human expression. “Incorrect. You see, I carry within my briefcase the epitome of my race’s technological advancements, having already collected all of your race’s finest achievements and sent them back to my planet. It is called an *illythrin’quirri*, a molecular diasporator. Know that we have been aware of this gradual diminishment of universal speed for some time and, after mapping certain galaxies, deemed this galaxy the most expendable. The molecular diasporator will set up a chain reaction on this planet that will move from planet to planet, from solar system to solar system, eventually annihilating the entire galaxy in a burst of super-heated plasma. It is our hope that the universal loss of mass will prolong the life of the universe long enough for our people to discover a permanent solution to this problem.”

Dr. Dalen turned to Dr. Sajadein and noticed, with not a little annoyance, that he was smiling.

"Your people will do nothing of the sort," Dr. Sajadein began, "for, you see, I knew of your tamperings. That is why I arranged for a similar 'messenger' in another galaxy to counteract the effects of yours. Nothing as subtle as yours, but, at this moment, a little rocket, remarkably similar to your molecular diasporator, is in the final stages of landing. It should hit a distant galaxy—Nari-Gamma, I believe it is—within a few minutes."

Dr. Dalen hissed and picked up his briefcase. "You are a stupid, arrogant race, and it will be my greatest pleasure to annihilate you. It was I who, through the use of subliminal messages, told you to target a specific planet in Nari-Gamma. The planet you chose was mine. I communicated with my people the exact coordinates of your little 'messenger', and it has already been eliminated. Now, all that remains is the briefcase."

Dr. Dalen opened his briefcase and removed an opaque, dusty-gray sphere. Upon his touching it, it became luminous and began to glow with an eerie green light, revealing a mass of writhing fibers within. Placing it upon the podium, he was reaching his hands forward when he heard Dr. Sajadein whisper something, almost to himself. Dalen looked up and saw that familiar look of arrogance upon Dr. Sajadein's face.

"Liar," Dr. Sajadein whispered again, this time with an air of conviction. "You lie to us. You have not intercepted our missile at all. How could you? You yourself said that you communicated the coordinates of my missile to your people, but that is impossible, because your message would have to have traveled faster than light. Also, you said that you just sent a probe to your planet containing the information of our race. If you could somehow communicate this missile information to your race at such a fantastic speed, why not just communicate our race's history along the same lines? Why bother with a probe at all?

"You must be bluffing. You are frightened and want to eliminate our galaxy along with yours! I never trusted you, and upon learning that you'd be holding this dinner, I took the trouble to make a small purchase. I will not . . . *cannot* allow you to do this!"

Dr. Sajadein reached inside a pocket within his tuxedo and pulled out a gun.

4 minutes

Dr. Dalen took a step back, his tentacles thrashing wildly as Dr. Sajadein stepped up on the stage. The room went deathly quiet as Sajadein turned to Dalen.

"I have no knowledge of your alien metabolism. Indeed, I do not know if this bullet will even have any effect upon your flesh. However, for the sake of my galaxy, I will take that chance."

Dr. Dalen took another step back and stared directly at Dr. Sajadein. "Does it matter if I tell the truth or lie? If my race has truly destroyed the missile, then why kill me? That would merely doom the entire universe. If I lie, then the universe's life would be momentarily prolonged, and killing me would serve no conceivable purpose for the human race. However, I can tell by your expression that you plan to kill me. This is why your galaxy was chosen to be destroyed. You humans have a tendency to allow your reason to become clouded by emotion. It makes no difference to me whether I live or die; I came to this planet prepared to die. However, before you kill me, let me tell you two things. One, my people have destroyed your missile. The speed at which the message was sent was the speed of thought itself, for I am telepathically linked with my people. Two, if the universe ceases to expand, you will all effectively be killed. You see, space and time are more interwoven than you think. As the universe slows, time slows with it. You do not notice this because, to you, time is a fixed rate. If time were to stop, you would not perceive it, because your perceptions would stop.

"When the universe begins to recede, time will begin to roll in reverse. Everything that has happened up to now in the known universe will begin to happen again, only in reverse. You people will remove the food you have just eaten, whole from your mouths. This will continue until the universe has contracted back into a super-dense atom."

Dr. Dalen began to walk toward the molecular diasporator when he heard the click of a firing hammer.

Dr. Sajadein began to smile, the look of a man who knows he is already dead. "Either way it goes, we are doomed," he murmured. "Thus, no matter what I do, I will die."

Dalen edged toward the podium. "You have a firm grasp of the concept, Sajadein. Either way, you are doomed. Spare the rest of the universe, human. No matter what your decision, you are going to kill someone."

Sajadein shook his head and looked back at Dr. Dalen. "Very well. I think I will kill you." He raised the gun.

9 seconds

Dr. Dalen noticed, from the corner of his central eye, that the scientists seemed to have accepted the fact that they were powerless in the matter and were watching the unfolding drama intently. Suddenly, his body stiffened, causing Sajadein to step back. "Yes . . . I have five seconds to touch the orb before the universe will cease to expand," he hissed. Calculating the distance to the orb, he leapt forward. A crack of thunder from the storm barely preceded the sound of a bullet exploding from a gun. He lost all sense of balance as a white-hot piece of matter tore through his nervous system. He crashed into the podium, sending the sphere careening to the floor . . . only now, the sphere was flying back to the podium, which was righting itself.

ABOUT THE AUTHOR

Atief Heermance lives in Columbia, Missouri, where he is a student at Hickman High School. He wrote this story while at Oakland Jr. High School, also in Columbia. Reading and writing occupy much of his time, along with computer programming and role-playing systems. Atief's academic interests include physics, astronomy, history, and mythology.

* *Reverse creation.*

Perhaps their stories *were* true . . .

The Eclipse *Bird*

by AMITY GAIGE

I don't know why, but somehow they always seemed vulgar to me. They flew about overhead, sliding upon the wind like paper airplanes. They gossiped among themselves without pause. The sea gulls, of course. Although I tried, I couldn't see why the crew valued the birds' presence. The crew fed them until they were stuffed full with scraps and bread crumbs from the galley. They were messy, too. The more food they were fed, the messier they became. Their screams radiated from every feather. I simply regarded them as freeloading nuisances.

My sail aboard the *Eclipse* was short. Short according to the measure of the sailors who stayed up every night to smoke pipes and tell sailing stories. Long to them was twice around the globe. I was to sail for three weeks. To a city-dweller, this was long. I knew from the moment I heard the sea gulls crying that I couldn't stand three weeks with them. That isn't insanity, is it?

Like almost every passenger aboard the 164-foot *Eclipse*, I was sucked into the sailors' stories. They took place on the lower deck after dusk began oozing onto the horizon. There in the cozy cabins one could hear the water splashing gently against the sides of the ship. I declare now that the storytellers must have used these below-water-level cabins for effect! The splashing and the gruff voices of the men drew me into a trance.

One story in particular resolved my curiosity about why the sea gulls were encouraged to follow the ship. It was a superstition among sailors that the brash gulls brought luck on the journey. This upset me. These grotesque birds were driving me crazy because of a silly superstition.

Still, the sailors continued to feed the sea gulls. One old sailor in particular, a man named Simon, made certain that the sea gulls got fed. He had feathery silver hair, unblinking black eyes, and eyebrows that arched over his eyes like the wings of a bird. But he was mysteriously withdrawn and silent. He shuffled around deck every day and was quite obedient, not a harmful man at all.

The first day I talked to him was actually at night. I was restless. Periodically, my head would roll around on my pillow, and my mouth would fall open while my tongue lolled out. I'd wake up with a very dry mouth. So I got up, frustrated, and threw on my robe. Barefoot, I pattered down the deck to the rail. The moon was a yellowish white crescent, smiling down upon the sea, vibrating with the waves. Young, spoiled, and fiercely independent, I explored the passages that wound among the sleeping cabins. I rounded the corner of a cabin and stopped. The sea gulls were hovering above the ship, as if waiting for something. They had fallen silent. Still, I glared at them distastefully.

To my surprise, out came Simon from his cabin, hands full of food. He began throwing it out over the railing one piece at a time. Curiously, each gull seemed to dive down in an order, catching a tossed scrap squarely in its mouth and devouring it, then waiting for its turn to come again.

I frowned, but then walked casually up to Simon. When he saw me, he looked embarrassed and stopped feeding the birds. The sea gulls resumed their positions high above the deck, embracing the air with white-silver wings.

"Sorry for surprising you," I said.

He nodded and kept his unblinking dark eyes on the birds. After a moment of silence, he threw up a handful of bread crumbs, and the sea gulls dove for them in a disorganized mass.

He saw my scowl. "Why don't you like them?" he asked me.

Raising my eyebrows and chewing on the inside of my cheek childishly, I answered, "They're messy. Noisy, too."

He looked hurt.

"Why do you feed them? Why do you lead them along all the time?"

He seemed at a loss for an answer. I laughed to myself, thinking he would not admit to a stupid superstition. A grown man like him! For shame!

Bashfully he stuttered, "They . . . they're just . . . just beautiful to watch."

I nodded my head and gave him an unbelieving

stare. "Sure," I said sarcastically.

He glanced at me, a frightened glance, and turned his face to the sea. Then he threw out the remaining scraps from a bowl by the rail, hurried into his cabin, and shut the door behind him. I laughed and said to myself, "I'd be ashamed, too, old man."

The gulls resumed their screaming as I retired to my cabin.

In the morning, I was awakened much earlier than I desired by the cry of the hungry scavengers. I also awoke with a scheme in my head. No longer would I stand for the sea gulls. I dressed and ran to the deck. I shooed them away with my boots and angry hollers. They only scudded to the other side of the ship. I ran to that side and flapped my arms wildly. They flew crying once more to the other side. While dashing back across the boat, I tripped and fell, sliding along the deck on my stomach. A sea gull had taken a seat upon the rail. Looking down on me, it made what sounded like a laugh. I became so furious I grabbed a metal doorstop that lay loose on the deck and threw it at the bird. A *thump* upon the gull's white breast, feathers fluttering in the wind, and the gull dropped lifeless into the ocean.

Laden with guilt, I dashed to the rail to see it swirl helplessly in the wake of the ship and then drift out of sight. The other sea gulls sensed my violent act and edged, screaming, away from the deck.

"That's right!" I yelled. "Go away! Go home!!" My anger flooded back into me. I knocked Simon's empty bowl into the water. "No food here! No more!"

For a few days, they kept their distance from the *Eclipse*. I secretly stole all the food from their scrap bowl and shooed them away each morning and evening. The calls of hunger became more distant, and I smiled at my success in ridding them from the sky. Then, one day, they were not there at all. They were not missed much on the ship, though some of the crew members wondered about it as they talked among themselves. I was happy. At last there was some peace. The soothing lullaby of the waves and the whistle of the wind were once again in my ears.

Suspicion about the gulls was overshadowed by something much more terrible. Simon was gone. It actually took two days for us to realize he had disappeared, withdrawn man that he was.

Many rumors floated around. Of course, the wildest were told by the old storytellers in the lower deck cabins. "He's turned into a fish," they'd whisper. "I've seen it happen before." Or, "He's been murdered. Someone has thrust him headfirst into the engine. Comes out like chopped hamburger. I've seen it happen before." No doubt the most plausible theory was that he'd fallen overboard, possibly in his sleep.

Everyone was anxious to get to port. We were only a couple of miles offshore now. It had been a most eventful trip. The passengers all leaned out toward land, squinting to see who could make out port first. A mother held the hand of a young boy who jumped up and down to see the land. "Wutsit look like, Mama?" He eagerly clawed at her dress, which billowed in the wind.

I was trying to absorb the last few minutes of salty sea air. My bags were sitting obediently at my feet, ready for the dash from the wharf to the train.

A young lady about my age, squinting in the breeze, was the first to holler, "There's the port! Yes, there it is." Land rose tentatively above the horizon.

A little later, as the *Eclipse* approached port, I heard the sweetness of a Spanish guitar and laughter in the narrow streets.

When we pulled up to the dock, the captain gasped. I followed his wide eyes to a man standing on the dock.

"Simon," I whispered.

There he stood, looking quite small and frail. When the boat docked, everyone ran out and gathered around him. He was already in the process of explaining his disappearance when I reached him.

". . . and then I, uh . . . woke up . . . I guess." He spoke bashfully, the way he did while talking to me.

"Go on, go on, you woke up . . ." urged the captain.

"I found myself in the water . . . I must have been sleepwalking." His eyes were no longer sharp and decisive. They were puffed and glazed and stared vacantly. Then he looked at me and started, his terrified eyes like those of a child who has just lost his mother.

"I, ummm, stayed in the water not for too long, umm . . . a schooner came by. The sailors pulled me in." He looked down at the ground.

The captain paused, then patted him enthusiastically on the back, saying, "We're glad you're safe."

Simon's hair wasn't silvery white anymore, either. It had a drab gray color to it. He looked sad. His gull wing eyebrows were flat and dark. He was a lost old man. I wondered if I was the only one who had noticed this change in Simon. I glanced around the group. I wasn't. One old storyteller with a frizzy beard stared wide-eyed at Simon. I could see a story brewing deep within him.

ABOUT THE AUTHOR

Amity Gaige lives in Reading, Pennsylvania, where she is a student at Northeast Jr. High School. She has won numerous awards for her writing. Her interests include ballet, singing, and acting.

Ask your father, not your mother.

Memoirs of a 13-Year-Old

by WILLIE TURNAGE

The year was 1980, a time of depressing change in our culture. The hippies were gone, the Olympics were in Moscow, and Reagan was elected. It also happened to be the most valuable year of my life. That year I learned what the world was really like, and I'll never forget the three rules I learned that I still use today.

"C'mon, Willie! Wake up! It's Saturday!"

That was my mom, the only woman on the planet who treated me like Beaver Cleaver.

"Mom, do we have to spend the whole day buying clothes?" Robbie piped in.

Robbie was my older brother who claimed three things in his life: 1) He knew everybody on the planet, 2) He knew everything cool on the planet, and 3) He knew everything. Unfortunately, he did have one advantage: at the age of ten he was bigger and stronger than my mother. And since Dad was a traveling salesman, he did practically everything he wanted to do: pushed me around, ate what he wanted to eat, never listened to Mom, pushed me around, pushed me around, and pushed me around. The only good thing about this was that I got more sympathy from Mom, and that's not much.

"Mom, can we go to the mall? Mr. Amazing will be doin' a show for TV at 3:00, and if we get there three hours early, we'll get good seats!"

"We'll see, dear."

Lesson #1: Always ask Mom. Never ask Dad.

Mr. Amazing ruled. He came on TV every day at 3:00 on Channel 17. He always did neat science tricks and taught me about spontaneous combustion in lysosomes. He tried to be funny a lot of the time, but he was rarely any good at it. This disappointed me a little, even allowing for the fact that I told worse jokes than he did. He had two kids and never yelled at them or spanked them. I thought he was the greatest living soul within the vast expanse we call the universe—until I found out The Amazing Truth about him.

"Mom! Hurry up! We're gonna be late!" Mom seemed not to care about my life at all, unless there was something in it for her.

"What's your rush? Got a hot date or something?"

Mom? What if I did? What would you do then? Well? Well? You wait and see, Mom. I'll be married by the time I'm sixteen and then you'll be sorry. I'll come and visit, and you'll say . . .

"Oh, hi, Willie! Uh, who's this?"

"My girlfriend, Mom. She's pregnant. I'm the dad."

"WHAT! Oh no!"

Then Mom will start crying and slowly build up to

a bawl until she's screaming her head off in agony over this dreadful incident.

"Where did I go wrong, Willie? What did I do that encouraged you to do such an awful thing? Please tell me."

"You never let me see Mr. Amazing at the mall."

"WAAAAAAH!!!!!!!!!!"

"Don't worry, Mom. We'll get along."

Unfortunately, and unknown to me then, Mom was not that gullible.

"WILLIE! That's the third time I've called you. Once more and it's the board for you, mister."

Her yelling brought me out of my trance with a start.

"What do you want? I'm thinking and you won't even let me do that. Geez."

"Don't get smart with me, young man!"

Duh.

My mom loved to yell at me like that. It was like a God-given talent. I always seemed to think of a comeback, but I never said it.

Somehow, within the next thirty minutes, believe it or not, we got into Mom's car. This was the new car, a sleek Honda LX-I with automatic locks, a fuel-injected 4-cylinder engine, and power windows that I loved to move up and down, up and down, and up and down. The one disadvantage was that Mom used them against me to gain a sense of superiority.

"Mom, why'd ya do that?" My mother enjoyed this moment of power. She'd turned off the power windows, something she did often, destroying the only entertainment in reach for the next hour.

"Are we goin' to the mall?"

It was 10:23.

"Later, dear. First I want to go to the department store."

Yes, Mom, I know. She was setting a record. "Going to the department store" for thirty-four straight weeks. And every week the same routine—first the lingerie, then the skirts and blouses, and finally, to top it all off, belts and other accessories. I usually ended up doing one of two things: 1) Being a good boy and following Mom around or 2) Climbing on the mannequins. I preferred the latter, probably because I could relate to these guys. Besides, I could yell at them, and they wouldn't care.

"Willie, dear, come along. My, look at the lovely clothes on the pretty statues!"

Wow. I already know all of them, Mom. They're my friends, but I guess you don't know that! Let's see, there's Fred, Bob, Joe, Pierre, and Bru—

"HEY! WHERE'S BRUCE??!!! WHAT DID YOU DO TO HIM?"

The shock of realizing Bruce was gone terrified not only me but Mom, too, along with any other ladies within a fifty-yard radius. My anger brewed within like a pot of Maxwell House. I screamed at my mother and received a very stern look. Then it hit me: Mom doesn't work here. She couldn't have done it. It must have been the salesclerk! I dashed across the store in pursuit of the woman responsible for this felony. With the grace of Laurel and Hardy, I flung myself up on the counter right in front of the salesclerk, scaring her half to death.

"You! *You* took him! I know it was you! I HATE YOU! BRUCE WAS MY BEST FRIEND, AND YOU

KILLED HIM! WHAT?! HEY—WHAT'S HAPPENING? HELP!"

A hand was grabbing me firmly by the back of my neck and dragging me out of the store. "THEY'VE COME TO GET ME!!! STOP THE SLAUGHTER!!! SAVE BRUCE!!!"

The police weren't taking me away (at the time I wish they had). Mom was. That's worse. The next hour flew by; however, it was about five months before I could sit correctly again. I still remember the educating conversation Mom and I had.

"Why did you do that?"

WHOP! Spearheads of pain shot through me when the first blow hit.

"Why do you persist in embarrassing me?"

WHOP! WHOP!

I thought to myself, *World peace? Maybe not.* The pain had pretty much ended after the first thirty-two, so I didn't really care.

WHOP! WHOP!

"Don't you ever—"

WHOP!

"EVER—"

WHOP! WHOP!

"DO THAT AGAIN!!!"

By now Mom was more tired than I was. I think she got about thirty gray hairs and many wrinkles from this experience. She had to calm down. She was experiencing too much stress. She did have some compassion in her cold, frigid, tiny little heart, so I was treated a little more delicately the rest of the day.

It was now 12:03. Lunchtime.

I particularly remember the place we went to that

day, a Chinese restaurant called Bo Bo China. As we entered, Mom ordered. "We'll have one buffet and a kid's plate."

"Mom, why do I always get a kid's plate when I eat more than you?"

"To save money, dear."

The man behind the cash register began to chuckle. Then it became a laugh, then an uproar. Why was he laughing? Was he laughing at me? Was it something I did? Something I said?

Lesson #2: At all times, weasel your way out of paying extra money. Put on a nice face during the whole thing, and don't be affected by people's reactions.

The lunch conversation was a strange one, but that's to be expected considering this was my first exposure to Chinese cuisine.

"Mom, what's this black gunk?"

"It's Moo-Goo-Gai-Pan."

"Oh." I knew that, but what *was* it?

My mind pondered her words for many minutes. Moo as in cow, Goo as in baby, Guy as in male, and Pan as in cooking utensil. Therefore, this concoction of food was a baby male cow cooked in a pan. I could just see it, frying right there on the grill, and they actually *served* it to people!

My stomach was one step ahead of me. My dignity would be shattered if I let it loose, but I couldn't stop it.

"BBBLLLLLLAAAAAAAAAHHHHHHHHH!!!!!"

Three dollars of cow buffet all over the waiter.

Lunch ended, and Mom was still pretty ticked. It was 1:00. Hopes for Mr. Amazing were dwindling. He was probably already setting up! How could I ask

Mom whether or not I could go? She'd probably yell at me some more. Wait a second—I know! Do it subtly, an allusion, calm and casual. Wait. I'd tell her that I did everything that morning just to show how much I loved her. I'd made my bed. I'd given the waiter a napkin to help him clean up. Then I'd ask. But she'd just think I was greedy and only wanted to use her as a taxi to and from the mall. Come to think of it, that *is* all I wanted.

"Mom . . ." The tension grew. Sweat trickled down my forehead and into my eyes. How could I say it? Come on, mouth! Speak! "Uh . . . forget it."

I chickened out. My only hope of ever seeing my hero, and I wimped out. What had become of me? Soon they'd be coming to take me away to the State Home for the Wimps. My family would reject me, my friends would hate me, and I would never see Mr. Amazing . . . ever. People would rather read *The Enquirer* than come visit me. But wait—there was a light at the end of the tunnel, an idea that grew bigger and brighter!

When in doubt—"Go!"

"MOM! I have to go to the bathroom really bad! Could you please pull over?"

"It can wait till we get home."

This woman was on to me. "No, I have to go—" we hit a bump at 60 m.p.h.—"REALLY BAD!!!!"

"Well, OK."

We pulled into the next Texaco, which happened to be only one-half mile from the mall, and I made a run for it. I ran with all my might, running and running, never looking back to see what kind of horrid expression would appear on my mother's face. And there it was, closer and closer, my goal, the place where he was: North Town Mall.

It was now 2:00.

Panting and heaving, I flung the doors open. Desperate to find a good seat (one that my mother wouldn't spot), I ran up and down the aisles, knowing she'd be there in approximately ten minutes. I found a place behind a big palm tree and waited.

Nine minutes later (she must've been rushing), I saw her eyes fixed on my little, innocent, helpless, cowering body. The eyes flared with flame and anger worse than any bonfire thrown by a school with tons of spirit.

I was torn in two. My mind said, "Stay here. You were bad. Face up to your punishment." My body, on the other hand, knew better. "RUN FOR YOUR LIFE! I ENJOY LIVING!"

In a state of panic I darted under the seats, groping for some sense of direction. Spinning in a whirl of confusion, I ended up at the end of an aisle, with Mom at the other end. Luckily, I didn't have to fight crowds. She did. I managed to avoid her in the Children's Outlet for several minutes, Babbages for several more minutes, and, finally, Spencer's (an educational store).

It was 2:55.

The clock. Was it right? Could I be missing him, the whole reason I was risking my life? (I loved this guy.) Was I going to miss him? Heck, NO!

The race was on. People gave me weird looks when I began yelling, "DON'T START WITHOUT ME!" Apparently, Mom had sent Security to look for me, too, because there were two cops on my tail. (Mom's a Baby Boomer. She experiences too much stress. I wonder why?)

I made it back just in time. There he was, glimmering in the light—Mr. Amazing! I lived to touch the hem of his sport coat! That beige corduroy sport coat that symbolized everything he did. And YES! He was wearing his tie, the blue one with the red pinstripes. His hair was combed back, the style definitely familiar. I stood there in awe for what seemed like hours.

"MR. AMAZING!!! MR. AMAZING!!! DON'T START YET!!! WAIT FOR . . . ME!"

During my state of hysteria, I had unknowingly run up on the stage, yelling.

Lesson #3: No matter who it is, never upset an apparently calm adult and expect to get out of it without a scratch.

"IT'S YOU!" I screamed in a frenzy.

"Of course it's me, kid. Now go sit down like the others."

"Don't you know me? Willie Turnage! Your biggest fan! It's ME!!!"

"Yeah, I've heard it all; get him off the stage."

"What? You . . . you . . . MOO-GOO-GAI-PAN!!!"

He did remind me of that pile of black gunk I ate at lunch; never before had I experienced such disappointment. Most kids mature at ten or eleven, but I matured right then. My life was ruined. I never looked up to anyone again. Then I had to face Mom.

Yep, that's about it. I got over it within a year or two. Since then Mom has become a happy housewife and settled down. Mr. Amazing has been canceled, and I still remember my three rules. Most stories have a moral, or are supposed to have one, so here's mine. I'll tell it to you straight so your English teachers don't have to ask you to find it:

Ask your father, not your mother.

Never give away more than you have to.
Never interfere with adults.

ABOUT THE AUTHOR

Willie Turnage lives in Garland, Texas, where he attends Garland High School. Among his interests are acting (he's performed in community theater), writing, computers, and model building.

It was a summer of goodbyes.

Summer's End

by JEANINE SKENDZEL

Our rusting station wagon faithfully rolls past the monotonous wheat fields. The billboards are now less densely grouped from mile to mile, forcing me to stop counting them out of pure boredom. Fifty-seven signs ago we were home in Landview. Now we're heading to our cottage on Scenic Lake. A dull ache pounds in my head, and my stomach churns in rhythm with the motor. I stretch out comfortably halfway across the seat until I accidentally hit my sleeping sister, Tracy. Just a few months ago we could hardly fit in this back seat: that's when my brother, Drew, was here. He would take up half the seat alone. The pain stabs me and the memories quickly flood back.

We're diving for Drew's waterproof wristwatch as we do every year. One of us throws the watch as far as possible and the other person dives to find it. Since Drew is seventeen and I'm only fourteen, he holds an unfair advantage, but I never complain. This time it's my turn to throw it. He has already beaten me three times today by thirty seconds each, so this particular time I secretly throw the watch behind me. Drew bobs up and down the dock, searching for a glint of silver in the hot summer sun.

"Come on, Ben! What'd ya do with it?" he frustratedly whines. I foolishly grin back, pleased that I have finally outwitted him at something. Grabbing my arm, he strongly twists it into a horrible snakebite.

"Tell me, Ben, or you know what's coming," he whispers, checking for our parents. We glare at each other, flashing our ugliest poses. Finally, we break down laughing, and I point happily toward the watch.

"You little . . ." is all I hear before he sprints off the dock and pulls into a flawless dive.

Usually he's able to grab it right away, but this time he remains underwater for a long time. I move down the dock to where I'm standing directly above him. He isn't squirming and his hand isn't groping. I figure he's getting me back for tricking him, showing off how much better he is than me. But then I notice his head curved in an awkward position, and I realize he isn't joking. Frantically I jump into the cool, neck-deep water, momentarily stunned and unable to help my own brother.

"Mom! Dad! Come quick! Something's wrong with Drew!"

Both my parents run wildly over. Dad pushes heavily through the water and Mom's feet pound on the rickety dock. Mom falls to her knees, weak and faint as she spots her son crumpled on the bottom.

"Ben!" Dad shouts. "Hold his mouth above water while I call . . ." Then he's gone, bounding up to our cottage, three steps at a time.

Drew's skin is cold and leathery, even though it's eighty degrees out. I feel sick and I notice my hands trembling, shaking Drew's fragile head. I can't believe this is happening. I can't believe it . . . I can't believe it . . .

"Move it, Ben! You're squishing me," Tracy shrieks, pounding my shoulder with her fists and pulling me back to the present. Tracy's only seven years old and doesn't understand anything yet.

"Sorry, Trace," I mumble and slide back against the vinyl door. Normally I would punch back, but I don't want Tracy to notice me crying and tell Mom.

Blankly I stare out the window again. I start counting the cars that pass us. One . . . two . . . three. An ambulance with bright flashing lights pushes in front of us. Dad calmly eases on the brakes. Mom jerks her head up from dozing, then slowly drifts off again. Dad reassuringly puts his hand on her leg, then continues on, picking up speed. The ambulance triggers emotions in me, igniting my memory once again.

"Drew Monroe. M-O-N-R-O-E."

"Ah yes," the nurse booms, flipping through some papers. "Drew is being treated in Room 203. You may see him but please remain quiet. He's reported to be in very critical condition."

Our family nervously moves toward the elevator. Everyone smiles, as if they understand the torture our family is experiencing. Even the elevator purrs calmly, steadily rising. The doors open and push us out on the second floor.

A nauseating smell hits me hard, making me clench my stomach tight so it won't flip over. People busily scramble in all directions. We pass by halls and halls of rooms, all the same. From a nearby room, a man gasps and screams out in pain. I creep by, curiously stretching my neck inside the door. I can see many doctors surrounding a bed. But as I shift my weight to walk away, they break their huddle and pour into the hall.

They flit past me, leaving the room empty except for a barren figure covered by a clean white sheet. Everyone is seemingly unaffected, and the bustle continues as if nothing has ever happened.

Walking on, I count the floor tiles, praying that before I reach one hundred, the floor will swallow me up and place me back in a normal life. I look up and see the door, Room 203.

No one in my family says anything. Our shoulders sag, yet our muscles wait in tense anticipation. Our drooping bodies give a clear picture of our emotions.

We enter. A machine sadly beeps out his vital signs. There lies my brother. Tubes and wires connect in a maze of circuits all around him. A machine is helping him breathe and blood hangs from a bottle on the side, slowly dripping life into Drew's muscular arm. His face appears lifeless and rigid, not anything like the Drew that I know. I can't stand to look at my brother in this kind of shape. In tears, I turn toward the door. No one tries to stop me. They let me walk out of the quiet room and into the large corridor filled with bustling life. Dizzily, I stumble through the hallways and down the stairs until I find the entrance. Reaching the outdoor air, I sink down against the brick building, crying and crying for my brother, Drew.

I never went back to the hospital again. I'd think

up excuses to stay home.

"I'm sorry, Drew, that I never came to see you, but I was scared, so scared," I whisper.

"What, Ben?" Dad breaks in. "I didn't hear what you said."

"Nothing, Dad. I was just talking to myself."

"OK, Son," he replies and turns back to his driving, apparently satisfied with my answer.

I glance around at everyone in the car. It's hard to believe we're still together. It sure was difficult at home.

Slouching back, I begin to doze again. My mind paints a picture of our house back in Landview. We'd stayed at home the rest of the summer to be near the hospital Drew was in. Yes, it sure was hard at home . . .

"Everyone ready to go see Drew?" Dad shouts from our front porch. I remain on the kitchen stool, polishing off my third bowl of Fruit Loops. Tracy joins Dad outside. She doesn't really understand what's going on, but is beginning to ask questions about why Drew is hurt and when he will be coming home. She can feel how sad our family is now, and she's becoming noticeably more irritable every day. Mom and Dad have been very lenient with her lately, too, which isn't helping her already-spoiled attitude.

"Carol, come on. We're leaving." Dad waits at the car door with Tracy hanging at his side.

Dad's been the strong, supportive one. Without him, I think we'd all drop instantly with nervous breakdowns.

"Ben, where's your mother? Aren't you coming with us?"

"I can't, Dad. Sorry. I've got things to do."

"Ben, I want you to come with us. Drew's your

brother; he needs you."

"He's in a coma! What does he know?" I yell angrily. Tears begin to well in my eyes. Immediately I regret what I said, seeing my father's hurt expression.

"Let Ben stay home," Mom whispers as she steps outside. Her eyes are puffy and bloodshot. She's changed so much since the accident. Usually her clothes are perfectly coordinated and her hair is carefully set, but now she appears ragged and worn. Yawning, she unconsciously pulls on Drew's summer jacket.

"Carol, that isn't your coat," Dad calmly states. His face is scrunched in concern. I know that he's worried about Mom as much as he is about Drew.

When Mom realizes whose coat it is, she breaks down in tears and rushes back to her room, slamming the door behind her. Lately all Mom ever does is lie in her room and cry. I worry so much about her.

Dad rushes after her, attempting to soothe her with gentle words. The two walk out hesitantly, arm-in-arm, to the car.

I place my dirty dishes in the overcrowded sink. Since Mom isn't doing any housework and Dad just doesn't seem to notice the terrible mess, our house has become a pit. I wade through the heaps of junk in the living room and hurry to my own room.

The car slows as we drive into a town, and I ease wearily back into reality.

"Hey, everyone, we're in Plainfield," Dad says, trying to sound enthused. "Only five more minutes to go."

No one answers him, although I think everyone heard. We pass by our friends' cottages. The car continues steadily past the beach at Scenic Lake. People wave to us and old familiar faces smile. Dad waves politely back, but Mom's face remains stone. She stares straight ahead as if we're on a dangerous mission.

Finally we arrive at our cottage. Everyone wearily steps out and picks up a suitcase to carry inside—everyone except me. I stiffly walk down to the dock. It seems like ages since we were here last. I wish we were back in Landview.

I glance up at our cottage. Tracy is at the study window, watching me. I frown, because the study brings back painful memories. We have a study exactly like it at home, and I think about the time Dad called me in for a talk. I think about how I sat, swallowed up in Dad's leather couch, knowing it was important because we kids were never allowed in this study. I tried to recall having done something wrong that I would get in trouble for, but I couldn't think of anything bad or out of the ordinary.

Finally, Dad walked in. His head hung low, and when his eyes met mine, I noticed that they were red and puffy.

"Ben, son, this is very hard for me to tell you, so please be patient." He wiped his eyes with an already-damp handkerchief. "Your brother was so good, and I know you loved him just as we all loved him—very much. We've got to work together as a family to help each other through this tragedy, because we need you, Ben, and you need us." He could barely speak without choking. I'd never seen him act like this before.

"What is it, Dad?" I was so scared. I began to cry before he told me, because, of course, I already knew. He pulled me close and hugged me tight. My ribs ached and it was hard to breathe, but I clung to him even tighter, praying that what I had been thinking was wrong.

"Ben, Drew died early this morning."

Drew died early this morning . . . Drew died early this morning . . . The words echo through my head as I stop at the exact spot where Drew dove.

"Why did I have to throw the watch *there*?" I whisper. "If I hadn't done that, Drew would still be alive now." I begin to cry again, but this time I cry even harder and everything inside of me hurts. I kneel, my knees digging into the sharp corners of the dock which press deep marks into my skin. My head aches from the pressure and heat of the day. I feel as though every muscle is screaming for a whole night's rest without tossing and turning or reliving painful nightmares. But I hardly notice the physical pain; it's what I'm feeling in my heart that hurts the most.

Through the rotting cracks between the boards, I glance down to see the lake's clear bottom. The glint of steel catches my eye. The watch I'd carelessly thrown in for Drew still lies there, half-covered by sand. I wiggle out of my torn T-shirt and take off my shoes and socks. With only my shorts on, I slip into the cool water and lift the watch from the bottom. I pull it close to me, clasping it tightly with both hands as I surface for air. I pull myself back up onto the dock. The watch is still ticking and in good condition.

"Drew, I'm really going to miss you," I whisper, scraping off the loose sand covering the watch face. Slowly I wrap it up in my T-shirt, making sure it's secure.

Rising to my feet, I wipe the tears from my eyes. Fresh tears insistently seep back as I trudge up to our cottage, ready to help unpack again.

ABOUT THE AUTHOR

Jeanine Skendzel lives in Traverse City, Michigan, where she attends Traverse City Sr. High School. She enjoys athletics, particularly basketball, long-distance running, tennis, and skiing. She reports, "My second home is the gym." Jeanine wrote "Summer's End" while at Traverse City Jr. High School.

Happily ever after despite themselves.

Chauvinist Knights and Feminist Damsels

by SELENE SMITH

"I won't marry that wretched Lord Kevin!" Kayla stormed out of the room and down the stone corridor. Her gold-red tresses streamed behind her, and, without breaking her stride, she grabbed two big handfuls of dark green velvet and hitched her skirt up above her knees to keep from tripping.

As she ran to her chamber, she could hear her father in the dining room where they had been eating dinner. She heard his chair scrape against the polished floor as he stood and moved heavily to the door.

"You *will* marry Lord Kevin, and you *will* be happy!" he bellowed.

Kayla stopped around a corner, breathing hard. As she listened to her father continue his tirade, she reflected on the inconvenience of women's clothing. She decided that she would much rather dress like a man, at least when she was moving about.

"It's time you grew up and left your tomboyish

ways behind!" continued her father. "I won't have you embarrassing me like this again, do you hear? Just be glad that your husband will be a rich and powerful lord who can get you anything you want!"

"Too bad I can't stand him," she said to herself. She flipped off the bothersome heeled shoes that were way too small for her large feet, gathered up her skirt, and began running down the candlelit hall toward her room. Her bare feet slapped against the old stones, but she paid no attention. Tears stung at the back of her eyes, but pride kept them from falling.

She slammed her door shut and flung herself onto the high, canopied bed. How could Father do this? Couldn't he see that Kevin was an egotistical and chauvinistic little wimp? Didn't he know he was committing her to a loveless marriage with a man she utterly despised? How could he give his only daughter away to a gold-hungry man who spent most of his time in front of a mirror, greasing and curling his moustache? Surely Kevin was already gloating and bragging about some exploit to prove his manhood: it was expected that a man requesting to marry the daughter of a noble would present a large treasure to the girl's father, and it was usually won in some sort of battle or journey.

What a crock, she thought. *I won't marry Kevin if there's anything* I *can do about it!*

Kayla, being not nearly as naive as women were supposed to be, knew that Kevin wanted her for more than her somewhat average prettiness. It was doubtful that he had fallen in love with her. That left only one reasonable answer: he wanted her dowry and the money that would be left to her when her parents died.

She thought, with grim satisfaction, that the person she despised most in the world, Kevin, was shallow. His motives were clear to her. But it hurt her deeply that her own father was just as shallow and transparent. He was obviously after the riches that Kevin would offer.

Kayla stood stonily between her parents and a little behind Kevin on the rough wooden platform in the town square. Her mouth was puckered, sourly showing her discontent, but her parents seemed to be smiling and waving enough for all of them. "Nobody knows," she whispered, looking over the crowd of people. "No one suspects that I could be unhappy about marrying 'the handsome Lord Kevin.' "

The city folk had gathered for two days of feasting to celebrate the engagement of their Lady Kayla to the dashing, foreign Lord Kevin, who was much admired for his fortune. This was the evening of the first day, and as the sun set over the mountains, Kevin announced his plans for an adventure.

"Halloo, good people!" shouted Kevin above the cheering. "As you all know, Lady Kayla and I will be joined in holy wedlock in one month's time!" He reached for Kayla's hand and pulled her close. Wrapping an arm around her waist, he waved a mug of ale in wide arcs with his free hand. Kayla bared her teeth in an animal-like snarl and tried to pull away. Kevin smiled drunkenly and tightened his grip. He continued his speech.

"I am here tonight to announce my plans to defeat the famous dragon that lives among these mountains."

He gestured with his mug and swayed uncertainly, spilling beer on the platform and on the hem of Kayla's dress. "I intend to confront that foul beast and bring back his treasure in exchange for this beautiful hand in marriage!"

The crowd *oooed* respectfully, hiding their disappointment. This was a task so often tried that they were beginning to be bored with it. Kevin, however, reignited their passion by lifting Kayla's hand to his lips. His hot breath smelled of rancid beer. She quickly snatched her hand away and wiped it on her skirt. She was disgusted, unable to imagine giving up her freedom to spend the rest of her life with this man.

Before she could protest, Kevin led her down to the center of the crowd where couples were forming, preparing for a dance around the bonfire. He took her arm, and they began to whirl and stomp with the others. Had it not been for Kevin, Kayla would have enjoyed herself. Dancing was one of the few lively activities that women were allowed to engage in, and she loved it.

But not this time. She could feel Kevin's sweaty arms on her; the combined odors of his ale and moustache grease mingled unpleasantly in the air around her face, causing her to feel woozy and nauseous. When the dance finally ended, she was relieved to find that Kevin had to hurry off and prepare for his journey.

She sat down on a bench near the fire to regain her composure. But soon she was surrounded by a group of young women from the village who sighed and gushed over her engagement. She smiled politely and gave only the necessary retorts to the questions directed at her. Then, as quickly as they had come, they drifted off to join other groups of merrymakers and soon forgot all about her.

She stared into the fire, listening to the sounds of people enjoying themselves all around her. Old men guffawed at funny stories told for what seemed like the hundredth time, young men raised cheers as they drowned their troubles in casks of ale, and mothers called to their children who were chasing each other through clusters of adults. Abruptly, her reverie was broken by a hand on her shoulder. Above her shone a pair of the bluest eyes, eyes that seemed to be laughing secretly at the whole world! They belonged to a young man she had never before seen. He was taller than the average man, with black, wavy hair and a clean-shaven face. He smiled at her gently and asked for a dance.

Gathering her wits about her, she nodded and stood up. He led her to the dancers, where they began to move to the beat of the music. Kayla was thankful that the constant movement kept their eyes from meeting . . . She might not be able to turn her eyes away!

They remained silent throughout the dance, and when they grew tired, they walked away from the crowd to the edge of the woods. The sun's last rays flickered and dipped. For a moment, Kayla wondered if she should say something to break the silence between them, but their silence was a comfortable one. She sat on a log across from the mysterious young man and gazed down shyly. Her fingers fiddled with the creases and folds of her soft white dress. She looked up when her companion spoke.

"So—you are duly excited to be engaged to the oh-so-elegant Lord Kevin?"

Kayla was not quite sure whether he was teasing or trying to be polite, but she suspected that he was laughing at her behind those mocking blue eyes. She felt her face grow hot as the flush moved from her neck to her cheeks, and anger boiled inside her. She stood abruptly and began to walk quickly in the direction of the crowded square.

A hand gripped her arm, stopping her mid-stride. She stared at this hand, a tanned hand contrasting boldly with her white skin. She could see that his expression had changed dramatically; now he looked unsure of himself, and almost sorry.

"I'm sorry if I offended you, but I couldn't help but notice that you weren't as thrilled with your engagement as everybody else was."

Kayla's feelings were suddenly mixed. On the one hand, she wanted to turn her nose up at this self-assured stranger and run. But, on the other, she knew she needed *somebody* to confide in. This unlikely person seemed to be the only one who even noticed her unhappiness.

"I guess I haven't been as happy as everybody thinks I should be." She half-smiled in an attempt to hide her feelings.

"I'd pity any woman who married Kevin."

"Then you know him?" she asked, startled.

"Yes, actually. I have the dubious pleasure of being his cousin. My name is Lance. And you, of course, are the ill-fated Kayla."

She nodded slowly, warning bells sounding. *Trust no man!* Look what Father had done to her! And Kevin was so odious! Surely this Lance, Kevin's own cousin, would hurt her in some way, too. But even as part of her warned against him, she felt deep inside that this man was different. The part of her that was walled off to others began to crumble before this stranger, whom she had known for scarcely an hour . . .

"At ease, men! You can all stay in camp. I won't be long," said Kevin importantly. The young men accompanying him showed their disappointment. They would like to have shared in the glory of a dragon-slaying.

"He just wants all the attention," one young man whispered to another. The other nodded in agreement as they fixed Kevin with their resentful glares. He didn't notice.

"If I'm not back in camp by tomorrow, send somebody up." His tone implied that this was not something he expected. He hitched himself up in his saddle and nodded at the men. Then he turned and rode off into the forest.

When he arrived at the cave, he tied his horse to an oak tree and unsheathed his sword. Any occasion to show off the jewels embedded in the golden hilt was welcome, even when he had only himself and the squirrels to admire it. He ran a hand over his hair to smooth it into place and twisted his moustache reflexively. Then he strode to the mouth of the cave, tripping rather ungracefully over a rock and cursing under his breath.

As he stepped inside, he was struck by a sort of swampy smell, and he began to feel a little afraid. "O great and fearful dragon, I *command* you to come out and do battle!" The challenge rattled uncertainly down the tunnel and died away, sounding more like a question than a demand.

He walked more carefully now, to avoid tripping. As he neared a turn, he could hear a deep, vibrating rumble. He pressed himself against the cold rock and waited, so filled with terror that his eyes were much rounder than seemed natural. He began to hiccup. Then, so slowly that he seemed not to be moving at all, he inched up to the curve and peered around the edge, ready to meet death face to face, but determined to see the fabulous treasure.

The cave opened up into a huge cavern lit by torches along the walls. Chests and barrels and bags were piled in huge drifts that overflowed with gold, silver, and gems such as Kevin had never before seen, and which his eyes greedily caressed.

Near the middle of the room, sprawled on a cushion of velvet and satin, lay the dragon. It was only slightly larger than a horse and covered with shiny brownish green scales that glinted in the torchlight. The tail was long and thick, like a huge spiked club, and was curled up to the creature's head. From there issued the terrible, jarring sound. The dragon was snoring.

Kevin pulled his head back around the curve and thought quickly. Maybe he could take advantage of the sleeping dragon and manage to come away with most of the treasure without even waking it! He had never actually promised that he would *kill* it; besides, outsmarting the dragon would still win him a reputation for being brave, daring, and quick-witted.

He sheathed his sword and crept inside the chamber. Then, turning his back to the rumbling beast, he grabbed a large bag filled to the brim with precious jewels. He began to drag it backward, but it was very heavy and moved slowly. So intent was he on his task that he didn't even notice when the dragon's snoring abruptly ceased. Frantically pulling to free the bag from a snag, he tugged and yanked until it ripped and sent him sprawling—right to the feet of the dragon. Cascades of gold pieces and rare jewels fell upon them both. Kevin saw his reflection in the golden cat-eyes of the dragon.

"Kayla, where have you been?"

Kayla saw the anger in her father's eyes and decided to tell the truth. "I've b—"

"No, don't even say it. You've been with Lance again. He's a nice enough young man, but you've been spending too much time with him these past two weeks. For heaven's sake, you're going to marry his cousin!"

At this, Kayla's mother, who had been pacing the floor, began to sob behind her hands. "It may be that Kevin will never marry anyone!" the lady cried, nearly hysterical.

Kayla looked at her father questioningly. He glared at her as if her mother's outburst was somehow Kayla's fault, then turned to comfort his wife. "We received word today that Kevin is being held prisoner by the dragon. There is a demand for ransom, and a meeting of the Lords' Council was called this afternoon to decide what to do." Kayla's mother, Lady Gwen, lost all control and had to be taken from the room by one of her ladies.

"And you decided—?" Kayla asked impatiently.

"We decided that we must send someone to take Kevin's place until we can gather enough gold to pay the dragon."

Kayla gasped in astonishment. "But who will you send? It must be somebody of nobility or there would be no assurance at all!"

Her father found it impossible to continue looking Kayla in the eye, and so his eyes shifted, darting here, there—everywhere but on his daughter. "I want you to understand that it was a very difficult decision, especially for me, but having examined every possible solution—" his voice petered out. He looked pleadingly at Kayla.

"No!" She took an involuntary step backward and raised her arms, as if defending herself from a physical blow. "You can't send me! You can't do this!"

"Kayla, sweetheart, there's nothing I can do. The Lords have decided. We need all of our men right now. It won't be for long, I promise." He tried desperately to comfort her; he hadn't realized how hard this would be.

She would not be comforted. She was angry, her eyes like knives that cut her father to the bone. "When must I be ready?"

Struggling to regain his composure and authority, her father croaked, "An escort will be sent tomorrow at dawn. It may take several days to get there, and you will need to bring some food and clothing."

Kayla turned her back to him and called over her shoulder, "Yes, I suppose I should, but first I am going to find Lance. He'll want to know. Don't expect me back too soon."

Her father hung his head and looked down at his

feet. He knew he'd been hard on her lately, but the truth was, he had been afraid to turn down Kevin's offer for fear he wouldn't get another. Now he saw it was possible for Kayla to make a match that would provide both wealth *and* love, or at least tolerance. "Kayla, I know you don't like Kevin very much, and I'd hate to back out of it now, but perhaps I can talk him out of this marriage—make an arrangement of some kind. That is, if you don't mind a little scandal. I want you to be happy."

Kayla rushed to his arms, all of her anger gone. Shining eyes and the glow of hope, so long gone from her face, filled the dark room with light.

Kayla stayed up late into the night, her maid packing her plainest dresses and strongest boots. Downstairs, the cook packed enough of her favorite foods to feed a party of young men for a month. She didn't expect to be gone that long.

In the morning, a procession of knights and nobles accompanied Kayla to the dragon's cave. Passing through small villages along the way, they were watched by peasant farmers and their wives who came out to line the roads. Kayla resented their stares and the air of excitement. She felt as if she were on display and the cause for a holiday or celebration.

She held her head high, her features composed to mask her inner thoughts. After a mile or two she felt as if her skin were concrete and about to crack. She tried to block everything from her mind except the rhythmic click of the horses' hooves, but Lance's face kept arising within her. She remembered their conversation from the night before, when she told him of the Council's decision. He had clenched his fists until the knuckles were white and his eyes turned wild. When she closed her eyes, she could still feel the warmth of his arms around her and the pleasant roughness of his shirt against her cheek. But then she opened her eyes and she was still on her horse, headed for the dragon's lair.

Kevin sighed heavily with relief when he heard hoofbeats and voices outside the cave. His first thought on seeing Kayla being brought ceremoniously into the cave was that his lovely fiancée had come herself to bring him home.

He approached, smiling, and took her hands in his. For once she did not back away from his touch but seemed to cling to him, reluctant to let go of part of her world. He noticed her nervousness and misunderstood it.

"It's all right, Kayla. Soon we'll be out of here—and married! Just remember that this is only an adventure of our youth," he said gently as he stroked her hands.

She looked at him sadly, and it occurred to her that beneath his chauvinistic exterior he might not be as bad as she had thought. She opened her mouth to tell him the truth, but before she could speak, her father came between them.

"Kayla will be staying here in your place, Kevin, until we get the ransom together." He took a deep breath, drawing inspiration from the piles of gold he imagined as a bridal payment from Lance. But then he remembered his promise to Kayla. "I think we'd better have a talk about the marriage. You might wish to reconsider . . ."

Kevin's face showed his hurt and disappointment. Kayla, instead of feeling the freedom she had expected, was embarrassed and ashamed. She hadn't meant for her father to humiliate Kevin publicly, and a dragon's cave was hardly the place to discuss his future, especially considering all that he had been through.

"Kayla can't stay here! I won't hear of it! Take her back at once! You can't expect me to let a woman stay here by herself."

She took a deep breath to control her rising emotion and stepped forward. "No, Kevin. You go back with them. They need you. I'll be fine." Her voice was confident and her eyes gleamed with stubbornness. He began to argue, but the men in the rescue party insisted on leaving the cave immediately. Kayla could hear his protestations growing fainter as they led him away.

Life with the dragon was not as bad as Kayla had thought it would be. At first she felt very angry, and to cover this she snubbed the dragon who, in turn, sat silently, staring at her. This doubled her anger, and she had all she could do to keep from screaming at the creature.

A small, gnomelike man who could not or would not speak, and whom Kayla assumed to be a servant of the dragon, showed her to a small side room off the large cavern where she made herself comfortable in the various velvet and satin robes scattered throughout the cave. With water drawn from a nearby stream, she worked hard to clean the area, then spent hours carrying in blankets, pillows, and even a small table and chair, inlaid with gold and silver.

After this labor, Kayla was too exhausted to feel angry. Although she hated to admit it, she was curious about this famous dragon who was said to be the most ferocious of his species. Unable to contain her curiosity, she wandered back to the dragon's apartment and sat down on a barrel well across the room from this mysterious roommate. She waited respectfully for several minutes to be spoken to, then, growing impatient, decided to risk starting the conversation.

After clearing her throat loudly to gain his attention, she introduced herself. The dragon nodded his head in affirmation and watched her expectantly. She had always felt that the only way to get things done was to get straight to the point, and so she did. She began to ask the dragon many questions; with a humorous twinkle in his eyes, the dragon answered her without hesitation. She began to feel comfortable and almost trusted him.

It turned out that the dragon was very considerate, and did not mind at all when she poured out her troubles with Kevin, her father, and Lance. He sympathized and agreed with her appraisal of Kevin. He did not think her foolish or immodest for discarding her heavy garments in the heat and going about in only her loose cotton pantaloons and shift. He let her sit in the sun on sunny afternoons and accompanied her on evening walks through the woods.

If truth be known, the dragon was well past his

prime and no longer pillaged surrounding villages as he had in his youth. He was actually glad for the company of this cheerful young girl to keep life interesting, and she began to think of her time with him as a vacation rather than a prison. They agreed that they would miss each other when the ransom was found. But that would be a while yet.

One warm afternoon Kayla was sitting in the cushiony moss under the spreading arms of a huge old oak tree, weaving a garland of flowers for her hair. The blossoms were dark purple-blue stars, the same color as her eyes, and the leaves were a rich, glossy green. She had just washed her hair in the stream, and it hung loose and damp down her back. She was humming to herself and didn't hear the footsteps until they were very close behind her. She stopped humming and spun around.

"Lance! What are you doing here?" Lance put his finger to her lips and pulled her behind the shelter of the tree.

"Kayla, are you all right?" He held her tightly and she was very aware of his touch, sure he could hear the hammering of her heart as she looked into his probing blue eyes. He had caught her unawares at her silly garlanding, and she blushed with embarrassment.

"Of course I'm OK—" *Now that you're here*, she wanted to add.

"I was so worried!" He ran his fingers through her damp hair. "Kayla, you have to go away with me! I don't have the ransom, but your father will be coming with it shortly. He has convinced Kevin that marriage to you would not work in the long run, but, well, Kevin did throw a terrible fit at first and there's a lot of talk. Your father and I thought it would be best if you and I stayed away for a while until things cool down. I realize that it will be difficult for you to leave everyone; your family and friends and all—"

"Difficult! Don't be silly. I'd give anything to get away from home for a while, away from all those busybodies and their opinions." She blushed and lowered her eyes, then looked up again. "It will be wonderful to be away—with you!"

He smiled at her, obviously relieved. "First, though, we'll have to decide how to deal with the dragon. If he doesn't let us go, I guess I'll just have to fight him."

"Don't even think of it, Lance. Let *me* talk to him. I'm sure he'll understand; he's actually quite nice and I've told him all about you." A skeptical crease appeared in Lance's forehead. "Don't worry. Really! I'm every bit as capable as you to deal with it."

He smiled at this and relaxed a little. "I'm sure you are. In fact, you'd probably be better at it than I. Off to talk to the dragon, then!" And away they went to the dragon's lair.

He didn't seem at all startled to see Lance. He just nodded his head stoically and said, "So you've come to take her at last. I was wondering what took you so long."

Lance's jaw dropped in astonishment, and so Kayla explained, "Yes, he has come, but he doesn't have the ransom. He says my father will be coming with it shortly. I hope that will be all right."

"Hey—no problem! That is, as long as the ransom is coming." He winked at that. "Come to think of it,

I haven't much use for gold now anyway. I already have so much! In fact, why don't you take some with you?"

Lance gave a little gasp. "I never dreamed it would be this easy or I would have come sooner. I was always told that dragons were mean, greedy animals who breathed fire and killed for the sheer pleasure of it."

"Well, I wouldn't have been nearly as nice if I didn't know Kayla would be happy with you. Don't cross her, though, and don't even suggest in her presence that women are weak, or *she'll* be breathing fire! She's a good girl who brings some spice into the life of an old dragon. But don't tell anyone—you might ruin my reputation." He winked again. "Now off with you before I change my mind and eat you both for dinner!" And with that, he dismissed them by closing his eyes and going to sleep.

ABOUT THE AUTHOR

Selene Smith lives in Bristol, New Hampshire, where she attends Newfound Regional High School. At school, she plays flute in the band and is a member of the track and field team and the cross-country team. Reading historical fiction, hiking, canoeing, drawing, and painting are some of her other interests. Recently she traveled to Italy with a college art group.

Some people are just so strange.

The Boarder

by JENNIFER GELBARD

I watched my daddy as he nailed the "Room for Rent" sign to the front of our house. It was summer again, the time of year when Daddy didn't earn as much, and we could use some extra money. Once again, he made our house available to any homeless stranger who could afford to pay.

We had already rented the room to many boarders, several men and one woman, Netty. Netty was nicer than the men. She was kind but poor, so to pay part of the rent she helped Mother with the cooking and cleaning. Netty loved our house. She'd stare at the ocean from her bedroom window for hours. Netty used to love the water. Now Netty was gone. She left two months after she came, but we never knew why.

I watched Daddy climb down the ladder.

"Should be gettin' someone soon," he said. "Makes me think of Netty. Remember Netty, Mindy?"

"Of course I do," I sighed. "Why'd she have to

leave us?"

"Don't know. That woman was just so strange. But sweet . . . real sweet."

"I loved Netty," I told him.

"We all did. Well, that sign's up. How's it look, Min?"

"OK," I mumbled. "But do we have to have a boarder this year, Daddy?"

"Do you want to eat?" he asked sternly.

"Yes," I replied disappointedly.

"Speaking of food, supper must be ready. Let's go inside."

"Wash up," Mother ordered as we entered the house. After Daddy and I scrubbed our hands clean, we sat down at the big oak table in the dining room.

"Lord," Father prayed as we all bowed our heads, "bless us kindly and thank you for the food placed before us. Hopefully, we'll find a boarder soon."

"And Lord," I added, "please make the boarder nice like Netty Holmes."

"Yes, amen," my mother, father, and sister, Lisa, agreed.

Lisa passed the potatoes to me, and as I took some I accidentally dropped a little on my new dress.

"I told you to keep that dress clean!" scolded Father. "Why don't you take care of your things? Get down on your knees!"

"I'm sorry, Daddy . . ."

"On your knees now!"

"No, Daddy . . . please . . . Mama . . ."

"Do what your father says," Mama said firmly.

"Get the water!" ordered Daddy.

"No, Mama!" I screamed. "I'm sorry!" Mother brought over the hot kettle of scorching water.

"Open your hands," yelled Daddy. "Now."

Hysterically, I opened my hands.

"Say it!" he yelled.

Shaking, I opened my mouth and said the words, "I was bad. I sinned."

Daddy poured some of the scorching water onto my palms as I closed my eyes tight. I screamed madly. My palms were now bright red.

"Say it again," demanded Daddy.

Lisa was crying now. "That's enough!" she shouted. "Leave her alone! It was an accident! Why do you do this, Daddy?"

Lisa made a big mistake by defending me. Daddy ordered her on her knees, too. At the same time, he poured water on our hands. We screamed. We cried. But it was the rule.

At last we were both told to go to our room and stay there until morning. On our way up the stairs, we heard a knock on the door. Could it be our new boarder? In pain but excited, we both sat on the top step and listened.

"There's a room for rent?" asked a tall, middle-aged man. He had a sweet expression, and he seemed very friendly and kind. He was shorter than Daddy, but then again, everyone was.

"Yes," answered Daddy. "A nice room. Real comfy."

"Oh," responded the man. "Sounds fine."

"Rent is sixty-five dollars a week. All right?"

"I think so," said the man. "Seems you're the only ones around here with a room so cheap. You're even right by the sea." He paused. "Well, my name's Bart

Hendricks. And you?"

"Darren Gray. And here's my wife, Vera."

"Charmed, ma'am." He tipped his hat, and Lisa and I giggled. "Can I be shown to my quarters?" asked Mr. Hendricks.

"I'll show him, Daddy," offered Lisa.

"Oh, Mr. Hendricks . . . my oldest daughter, Lisa, and my youngest, Mindy."

"Nice to meet you, girls. Now which one of you charming ladies is going to show me to the bedroom?"

"I will!" I shouted.

"Well, fine then." The new boarder picked up his two pieces of luggage and followed Lisa and me upstairs.

Daddy cleared his throat loudly. "Uh . . . aren't we forgetting something?" he asked.

What? I wondered. Suddenly, I remembered. The oath! The oath! We had been so excited about our new boarder that we had forgotten the most important thing of all.

"Oh no, Daddy!" Lisa begged. "No oath! He'll be good."

"Shush!" yelled Mama.

"Quiet!" Father ordered. He looked at Mr. Hendricks and laughed, as if this were pretty minor. "Mr. Hendricks, in our house we have a rule, not just for the children, but for boarders . . . any guest. If you do something bad or evil, although you may claim it is only an accident, the result is a scorching—just to show the kindhearted Lord that you're sorry. Now all you have to do is say, 'I'm willing to be scorched for my sins.' "

Mr. Hendricks was apparently shocked by this. He

glared at Lisa and me as if he were checking to see if it was all right.

"Go ahead," I assured. Lisa didn't say anything. I knew she never liked the scorching idea. Maybe 'cause it was a real original one. Everything with her had to be like other folks. She just frowned at Mama, and Mama put her finger on her nose, like saying "Be quiet."

Bart looked innocently at Daddy. "Are you . . . is this . . . ?" he started.

"Say it, Mr. Hendricks!"

"Well . . ."

"Say it!"

"I'm willing to be scorched for my sins." Mr. Hendricks said it real fast, as if it were a joke or something. He suddenly saw my red hands and gulped.

"Scorched . . . you mean burned."

"Doesn't matter now!" laughed Daddy. "You already swore to it!"

Bart looked extremely nervous.

"Come on, Mr. Hendricks! Let me show you the room!"

"All right, thank you . . . Lisa?"

"Yes, that's right, Lisa. Now let's go upstairs." Bart smiled. Lisa still seemed to like him a lot, but he seemed very strange to me.

That night, after we thanked the Lord for our home, Lisa and I got into our beds and Mama shut the light.

"Lisa?" I asked in the darkness.

"What, Min?"

"Why don't you like the scorching?"

"You do?"

"Well, I don't like getting the scorching, but what's wrong with having the rule? I think it's being very loyal to our Lord. When I grow up, I'm going to have the same scorching rule for my children."

"Well, I'm not! No one else does it. It's just so . . . so . . . dumb!"

"Stop it!" I yelled. "I'm going to tell Daddy that you said that. I bet that the Lord heard you! He'll punish you."

"It's just my opinion . . ."

"Well, it's bad!" Angrily I rolled over and went to sleep.

The next morning we woke up to the sweet smell of Mama's French toast.

"Wake up, Mr. Hendricks! Are you awake?" I yelled, knocking on his bedroom door.

Bart was in blue pajamas. "Girls! It's five A.M. What are you doing up?"

"What are you doing sleeping?" I asked.

"It's so early!" he exclaimed.

"You're so strange," I giggled.

"Mindy, stop that!" Lisa yelled. "That's not nice. Breakfast is just about ready, Mr. Hendricks. Won't you please join us?"

"That will be fine. I'll be right down as soon as I'm dressed."

Lisa and I set the table and waited for Bart to come down before saying the prayer. We sat patiently as our breakfasts got cold. At last a bleary-eyed Bart came down.

"Going to work today, Mr. Hendricks?"

"Yes, ma'am."

Mr. Hendricks reached for a piece of French toast and put it on his plate.

Daddy and Mama glared at the boarder as he gobbled it down.

"We didn't say the prayer yet!" I hollered.

"Mr. Hendricks!" Mother gasped.

"Eating without giving thanks. You're an ungrateful fool!" roared Daddy.

"Stop, Daddy!" yelled Lisa. "He didn't know!"

Mr. Hendricks dropped his fork on his plate. "Sorry," he remarked with his hands up. "I didn't know."

"Shame on you. You don't say thanks at home either, do you?" I scolded.

"Get up!" yelled Father.

"What's going on? I said I was sorry."

"On your knees!" screamed Daddy. "Vera, get the water." Mama got up and brought the kettle of steaming water to Daddy. Mr. Hendricks was flabbergasted.

"Wait . . . no! You can't do this. Heck, I'm not your child. What are you doing?"

"You took the oath!" I screamed. "You swore and now you've sinned."

Lisa was crying now, but I felt no pity for the strange man. "He deserves it," I whispered to Lisa. "It's wrong to be upset."

Daddy held Bart's hands tightly as he poured the water on them. Bart tried to get away, but no one ever could escape Daddy's grip.

That afternoon Bart silently walked into the house. He ran up the stairs, entered his room, and came out with his two suitcases. He walked downstairs to the living room where my family and I were seated. We all knew what was happening—it had happened before. He took his suitcases and left the house, expressionless. It was the same way Netty and all the others had left—quietly, right after their first scorching. We never could figure any of the boarders out. People are just so strange.

ABOUT THE AUTHOR

Jennifer Gelbard lives in Scarsdale, New York, and attends New Rochelle High School. She is an avid writer and hopes her readers will find a message in her stories. She has won various writing contests in her school and state. Jennifer wrote "The Boarder" while attending Albert Leonard Jr. High School, in New Rochelle.

Wanted: One pet duck.

In Search of the Elusive Wild Mallard

by SHAYNA GRAY

Being an intrepid type of person, one day in the spring I decided to go on a quest for that most elusive of birds, the wild mallard.

Now this was not as easy as it may sound to you, for the wild mallard, especially the hen, is loud and fierce and will bite to death if captured. They are masters of camouflage, blending perfectly with their natural surroundings. Sometimes they blend so well that you can pass right by one and never know she is there. But if you do find one, or happen accidentally to stumble upon one, the only thing to do is run for your life. Handling one of these irresistible creatures when it is aroused could cost you your earlobe, the tip of your nose, or your eyebrows. (That's if you're lucky!)

Anyway, this beautiful May morning I assembled the equipment necessary when searching for wild mallards: knee-high boots, fly swatter, large butterfly net, earlobe covers, bread ties, lettuce and popcorn, falconer's gloves, diving and swimming gear, and provisions for me. The boots, earlobe covers, and gloves are to protect the mallard-seeker when attacked by a vicious mallard; the popcorn and lettuce are to lure the hen from hiding (everyone knows they love popcorn); the net is for catching those mallards that try to fly away; and the swimming gear is used in case you must take to the water to catch the mallard. The fly swatter is for beating off hyper hens who try to chew your toes off or flap their wings in your face; and the bread ties are for closing shut the bills of biting birds and preventing unwanted tweezed eyebrows.

I decided to begin my search by the local river, which had acquired the nickname "Mallard River," making it a logical place to find ducks. It being early in the year, I thought I did not need mosquito repellent, so I didn't bring it, which was a really dumb move. I tromped along through the undergrowth, hoping for an early sighting . . .

By noon I was still looking! I was dirty, hot, tired, miserable, and covered with mosquito bites. I had fallen into the river twice, bumped my head three times on low branches, and after all of this I had heard only one quack. I sat down on a boulder and took out my lunch, a dehydrated concoction called "Trailblazer's Doom," and poured water into the package. I suppose it was all right, but the only thing I could think of that tasted worse was rotten tuna.

After I had finished my lunch and was preparing to drink the warm remains of the iced tea I had brought along, I heard a loud quack quite close to me. (By then, the choking and abdominal seizures had subsided somewhat.) I ran, rather, stumbled off the boulder in the direction of the quack. Just to be on the safe side, I donned my falconer's gloves, knee-high boots, and earlobe covers.

A steady stream of quacks led me to a willow-overhung sandbar near the south bank of the river. As I got closer, I heard the distinctive *chink* sound peculiar to mallard hens. By the sound of her I could tell she was broody, for the *chinks* were quite agitated. As the river was shallow here, I was able to ford it only up to my chin, and the undercurrent was weak enough not to drown me.

Before I even set foot on the slimy sand, the wild mallard hen saw me and took to the water. In the great tradition of sportsmanship, I dove in and followed her. She was a skillful swimmer, seeming to know just how to turn so that I'd bark my shin on rocks or fall face forward into slimy water weeds. The mallard, seeing she was only forty-five feet ahead of me, decided to take to land. I flopped out of the river (alas, I had forgotten my scuba gear) and kept up the chase. Luckily, all the slime rubbed off on the brambles I clawed through and the logs I tripped over. Mallard just kept on running nimbly. I was ready to give up and fall into a well-deserved coma when she decided to take to the air. I managed to grab her by her tail feathers, and we both fell into a thick, luxuriant growth of prickly sandburs.

As it turned out, I was more tired than Mallard, who seemed perfectly willing to display her teeth by imprinting them on my arm. She completely ignored the falconer's gloves and went straight for the upper arm area, which was extremely inconsiderate of her (I spent forty-eight dollars on those gloves!). However, I managed to tame her somewhat by tying her bill shut with the bread ties.

"At last!" I cried, holding her high in the air. "I have captured the wild mallard, the one that every hunter hunts in vain! Oh, little Mallard, you are the dream, the goal of brave, bold hunters everywhere; and I, I have captured you! Little Mallard, you are beautiful!" And despite the possible danger of losing my nose, I lowered the little duck and kissed her.

Mallard-seekers hunt fiercely for their prey for the satisfaction they receive when they finally catch one. These little birds look unbelievably adorable when held up in the air, their necks projecting downward, giving you a perfect view of their slightly pear-shaped heads, bulgy brown eyes, and twin, dark brown stripes running horizontally along the sides of their faces.

Most naturalists or mallard-seekers prefer to free their birds (knowing that the little monsters eat like horses and make more mess than a whole stable of them), but the mallard I captured was so cute I just could not bear to let her go, and thus decided to bring her back with me. I had no idea as to how my family would react, but I was sure they would be just as pleased with her (once they got to know her) as I was.

As we proceeded at a slightly more leisurely pace homeward, I got to know my little mallard quite well. She was really very gentle, enjoyed sitting in my hand, loved lettuce and popcorn, and ate Trailblazer's Doom with a lot more gusto than I did. I called her Helen.

My family did finally accept Helen, although once I caught my brother looking thoughtfully at a bottle of orange sauce in the grocery store. Helen liked my family almost as much as she did me, and they were very proud of my being able to catch and "bring back alive" the elusive wild mallard.

About the Author

Shayna Gray has been writing short stories since age six. She lives in Motley, Minnesota, where she attends Motley High School. Her interests include reading about the Arthurian Age, and she raises ducks. She has a pet mallard.

The doors of K-Mart part like the Red Sea . . .

Nightwalk

by ALEEM HOSSAIN

I walk alone in the velvety blackness of night. Ahead I see the parkade, an oasis of light to most. A raccoon scurries halfway across the road in a bouncy trot and then stops. It turns and looks me in the eyes as if it were my equal; I start to laugh, but don't, because perhaps it is. But then again, what does it know?

I come to the corner and look down the street—why I don't know, for I never see any cars on my way to the parkade. A house up the street is alive with voices and music. As I pass, I hear the heavy bass of the stereo, overlaid by a multitude of worthless people saying worthless things. But once again, who am I to judge? I don't go to parties; I'm not invited to any—not that I would go if I were.

I stop for a second to watch the clouds cover the moon. I whisper goodbye to it, lest it not come back. But it does, and I continue on, humming a long-forgotten song about love. This time I do laugh—I laugh at all the foolish people taken in by love's illusion. My laughing turns to heavy sighs as I cross the street, not bothering to watch for cars. It doesn't matter; there aren't any. I think of what Anthony would say if he were with me on this walk, but he isn't, and I curse myself for thinking of things that will never be. I'll meet Anthony at K-Mart as I always do on Friday nights. We'll roam the store, and when there's nothing left we'll part and go home. I shake my head and think how useless it is to walk this same lonely road every week. But I never listen to myself because here I am. Then I think about staying home and decide I'd rather be here. My mother wants me out of the house; if I stayed, I'd just sit around watching TV, probably Part II of some miniseries that nobody saw the beginning of, yet watch as if they know all about it. What fools! If Anthony were there, he'd change the channel and I would let him, even though I myself long ago gave up on attempts to make my family understand. I don't waste my time with them anymore, but I curse myself for being stupid and letting them just slip away.

I enter the warmth of a streetlight and stop to embrace it. Instinctively, I step up onto the curb and walk toward K-Mart. I stop at the entrance, lingering there for a long moment. I almost turn to leave but, realizing there's nothing else, I walk inside. The doors part like the Red Sea and I tell them I've never even seen Moses, but they're not listening. I turn to my right and hit the flier stand; I always do. The coupons fly everywhere, but tonight I keep on walking (not that I ever stop to replace them). I have no time to stop; my time is wasted enough on the useless things that make up my life.

I remember that I have to get my mother that glass vase, the one with the pink flowers on it. It's ugly and fake, but her $7.50 is in my pocket along with $3.00 for me, so I may as well buy it. I shake my head as I think about the vase but decide to get it. The fact that my mother wants me to get it has nothing to do with my decision; it will simply give me a reason to be here, a reason that I will not speak of but will use to deny the fact that all of this is pointless.

Anthony sees me and walks over to where I am standing. We greet each other; he really thinks I like him—which makes him so inferior—but I realize that this is just an illusion, and, besides, he is nothing to me. Or is he? I fight bitterly but cannot deny our friendship, so I begin to walk. He follows a second later, and we walk up and down the aisles. I look intently at all the junk and pause to consider many items; I'll buy something, I know that. Something useless, something, perhaps, befitting my character. We walk through rows of plants, and the smell of leaves and plant spray alienates my nostrils. I hate the smell but I walk just as slowly through this section as any other.

Anthony mumbles something about his lack of money. I tell him I have only enough for the vase. A lie, not even a necessary lie, but I tell it nonetheless—perhaps to once again trick myself into believing that I control him, rather than acknowledging the truth of his magnetism over me. I tell myself I would come here alone, even though I wouldn't. I'd never come inside just to walk around. But now I'm inside and that's what matters.

I stop and look at a red pen, a Bic Streamliner. It has a gray barrel with a red cap and body stripe. I stare at the pen for a long time, not actually looking at it but just letting my vision blur as I stare. It dissolves into a gray haze with little red patches, and I sigh. A tear rolls down my cheek; I don't know what for, but it does. I let it run all the way down my cheek, leaving a trail of hot, stinging moisture. I wipe it away just before it drops off my face: I will not grant it freedom. It is mine to hold and keep.

We continue on, not talking very much, just chatter about the ball game tonight, which I'm not really interested in, and other irrelevant things. Ahead of us is a huge candy display, a sugar citadel calling me forth from the streets of the store. I go to it and reach out for a bag of butterscotch drops. I hate butterscotch but for some reason I pick one up. Besides, it's only $1.99 and at the corner drugstore it would be $2.50. Anthony has looked at many things, but he has no money and is frustrated about it. He stares at the bag of candy in my hands, and his eyes fill with rage for a moment. I brush it off; who cares? An old woman passes us; she's wearing an old yellow dress that was probably white at one time. Around her neck is a mink, its head still intact and looking as if it's about to tear her shoulders to shreds. She eyes us suspiciously as she passes. Midway down the aisle she screams. I turn around and on her shoulder is a small dark spot which is slowly growing. I smile, knowing that it bit her good and hard.

I turn around and grab Anthony by the arm and jerk him in my direction. He resists for a second but then begins to travel the floor once more. We enter an aisle filled with Halloween masks. I look for one to wear next year—yet another instance of my useless wondering about the future. Then I spot one; it is a clear plastic mask designed to be painted on. I leave behind the paints and take the mask. Perhaps next Halloween I will put on the face of nothingness. Anthony finds a werewolf mask that he really likes but tosses it aside and catches up with me.

Then I remember the vase. I hand him my mask, candy, and wallet and tell him to wait here while I get the vase. I run to the glassware rack and find the pink flower vase. I grasp it and pause, for I know that once I take it I will rejoin Anthony and we will walk to the register, then out the door, where I will walk alone in darkness once more. I look down the aisle at Anthony—he is taking money from my wallet! I freeze as I watch him stuffing two dollar bills into his shirt pocket. I storm toward him, the store dissolving around me, a black vortex growing stronger and stronger as I approach him. My hands ignite as I reach into his pocket and grab for my money. But it's gone. I scream at him, shaking his body. He tries to defend himself but I don't hear him; I am too far above him.

Then he charges me and lands a punch right in my gut. As I keel over, my rage is once again sadness; in one blow my majestic rank is shattered, and the burning truth of who I am is no longer deniable.

"You have destroyed me," I scream, calling him a traitor. He stumbles back and starts to run. I command him to stop but he doesn't. He quickly bolts down an aisle of clothes. I follow him, passing a young child who tugs at a toy snake coiled around his neck. He looks up at me and I stare back. Immediately his expression changes and his face goes white as he coughs and gasps for breath. I smile as he wrenches the snake from his neck.

I continue after Anthony. I find him walking toward the door. I stop, thinking that he will not leave, that he will never leave. He slows as he reaches the door and then walks on through. I gasp and throw out my hands to him. The racks of clothes tower over me, casting their shadows. Suddenly I am lost in a deluge of falling objects. The vase hits the ground, and it shatters. I run for the Red Sea and pass through it, immediately engulfed in blackness.

I slow myself down and begin to walk home. Passing the house where the party is going on, I stop to stare through the windows. People are stumbling around inside, worthless people who fall through walls and don't even know it. I curse Anthony and try to believe that he never existed. Ahead, the raccoon rejoins me in the middle of the street. I stop and bow my head, waiting for him to pass. He stares at me, then slowly veers off the road. Once he is out of sight I continue my walk and reach my driveway. I jog up to the door, open it, and step into the cancerous atmosphere of my house.

On my way to the stairs, I grab the big butcher knife hanging from the wall. I pass my mother and she asks about the vase. I don't stop, nor do I answer her. I slam the door to my room and run my fingers up and down the cool, peaceful blade. I hold it to my skin, feeling its steel. Throwing off my shoes, I climb into bed with my clothes on. I reach for the blanket, needing its self-erasing blackness, but I can't reach it.

In a way, I don't really want its shaggy wool softness. Instead, I clutch the beautiful hard dagger against my throat. I pause, remembering the velvety blackness of a night I no longer have a place in.

I look out the window and see the raccoon staring in at me through the window. I turn away but finally face him. He cocks his head in a majestic pose, and suddenly I am looking up at him from far below. From my knees I tell him that he is my superior and that I will never again laugh at him. But then he too is gone, dissolved into night. I turn away and drop the knife, telling myself that it will be there for me tomorrow, and the day after, and the day after that.

ABOUT THE AUTHOR

Aleem Hossain is a student at Bolton High School in his hometown of Bolton, Connecticut. He enjoys writing stories and poetry, and he is senior co-editor of his school's literary magazine. Other interests include music, playing basketball and baseball, and collecting baseball cards.

Their love colored the sky . . .

The Story of the Aurora Borealis

by JAMIE PFLASTERER

Riotous laughter broke the night's calm and shook Mt. Olympus. Bacchus, god of wine and revelry and thus the favorite of the gods, had come to visit. As was Bacchus's nature, he had turned the rather dull gathering into a roaring Bacchanalia. It seemed as though his mere presence was intoxicating. Jove, leader of the gods, was out of control, which wasn't unusual according to Juno, his wife. He was running around with a huge chalice sitting upside down on his head and was flirting with all the goddesses. Neptune, god of the sea and Jove's brother, was accidentally sticking people with his trident while describing a fierce battle with an immense, bottom-dwelling killer whale.

However, not everyone was joining in the fun. Sol, former god of the sun; Luna, former goddess of the moon; and Aurora, goddess of dawn—dubbed "The Titan Triplets"—sat demurely in the corner. Sol and

Luna were there only because of perfunctory courtesy on the part of Jove and Juno. Since Saturn, former leader of the gods, and the Titans, his followers, had been overthrown by the Olympians, Apollo and Diana were regarded as the true god and goddess of the sun and moon, respectively. However, no one replaced Aurora as the goddess of dawn. She was a favorite among the Olympians. Rumor had it that she nearly rivaled the looks of Venus, goddess of love and beauty, when she smiled. However, that was rare since the terrible incident with Tithonus, Aurora's former lover.

Aurora had fallen in love with Tithonus, a mortal man, many thousands of years ago. She had taken up Tithonus from Earth, and they lived together at Aurora's home near World's End. Aurora knew, however, that their wonderful relationship couldn't last because Tithonus was mortal and would eventually grow old and die. She went before Jove and, using all of her charm, got him to agree to grant her one wish. She asked for eternal life for Tithonus, and her wish was granted. But poor Aurora forgot to ask also for his eternal youth! So Tithonus still lives; however, he has gotten quite old, and over the years he has shrunk and shriveled down into the form of a grasshopper. Aurora has been in constant mourning for him since, and has never loved another.

Aurora was quite shy. At the Bacchanalia, she had veiled herself in clouds and mists so that none of her could be seen, and she would barely speak to anyone who tried to coax her out of her little corner.

Suddenly, a chill spread throughout the vast room. Everyone turned around to see who had ushered in such an ill omen, and they all immediately relaxed again. Boreas, god of the north wind, had entered. It was only natural that one such as he brought a chill wherever he went. However, the feeling of unease never quite left the room.

Boreas floated around the room, lightly dusted with frost. Great icicles hung from his hair and clothes. He exchanged pleasantries with Jove and his court and then sat down on the fringe of the crowd. Unlike Aurora and Bacchus, Boreas was not a favorite of the gods. It was not that he was bad-mannered or unpleasant. He was simply too cold and distant for many people's tastes. Boreas didn't mind this. In fact, he preferred to be left to his own devices. He settled himself down in a chair and watched all the fun.

The gods and goddesses finally began to calm down and were becoming bored. As they were looking around for something else to amuse them, Proserpine, the young, carefree goddess of spring, spotted Aurora. "Sing for us!" she pleaded. "Call the dawn!"

Aurora looked away shyly, but a collective cry went up for her. Finally she walked demurely to the center of the room. The mists lifted, revealing a seemingly young girl clad in a simple homespun tunic. However, this young girl possessed an unearthly beauty. Aurora took a deep breath, opened her mouth, and began to sing.

Contrary to popular opinion, the dawn is not the rosy fingertips of Aurora. Instead, Aurora uses an ancient melody, older than time itself, to beckon the dawn back from its nighttime hiding place. Aurora weaves her powerful magic within the song itself and calls for the dawn to come back to Earth again.

All those sitting there were reminded of home and

their childhood as they listened to the song. A feeling of peace and security washed over the whole group. Then, right at the climax of the song, the first rays of light glittered across the land. Everyone hushed and simply took a moment to drink in the dawn and hold onto the memory of the song.

Aurora blushed deeply; everyone stared at her as she rushed back to her seat and again summoned the cloaking mists about her.

"Good gods!" Boreas exclaimed in wonder. "Never in all my years have I heard or witnessed anything so lovely!" Aurora's song had touched something deep inside him. He had fallen in love with her.

Apollo, god of youth, medicine, the sun, and music, among other things, was leaning on the wall next to him. He chuckled. "No doubt many of the others gathered here are saying the same thing. Although I am the god of music, she rivals even me at my best."

"Who is she?" Boreas breathed in awe.

"Don't you know? That was Aurora, goddess of dawn. She lives away from Mt. Olympus at the edge of the world."

"Of course! Now I remember!" Boreas was silent for a moment, lost in thought. Finally he said, "Apollo, I need your help."

Apollo drew his attention back to Boreas. "How may I assist?"

Boreas had formulated a plan to get Aurora's love. Now all he needed was Apollo's help. "Can you make me Aurora's equal in song?"

Apollo grinned. "You should be consulting Venus on matters of love instead of me." Boreas flushed. Serious now, Apollo frowned. "This is no small thing you're asking for."

Boreas looked panicked. "Please help me! I will repay you in any way I can!"

Apollo thought for a moment and then said brightly, "Could you trade me two of your coldest winds to keep me cool as I drive the chariot of the sun across the sky, in exchange for changing your voice?"

Boreas quickly agreed, even though his supply of winds was limited. Apollo then slowly began to change Boreas's voice to that of a great singer. In the process he also made Boreas taller and more handsome and godlike in appearance. Finally, the change was complete. Boreas thanked Apollo soundly. "I can never repay you for what you have done."

Apollo winked at him. "Good luck!"

Boreas saw the clouded goddess get up to leave. He pushed his way through the throng of gods and goddesses, trying not to lose Aurora. Outside Mt. Olympus, he saw Aurora, or rather, the stray mists trailing along behind her. It seemed that he followed her for an endless time, always trying to keep her in sight and yet afraid to let her see him.

Finally, she came to a cottage, modest by the standards of the gods. He didn't follow her inside, although he wanted to. He was too nervous to actually try to meet her face to face that night. He needed some time to think everything through once more. The sun had set hours ago, so Boreas prepared himself for a night outdoors—nothing unusual for the god of the north wind.

When Boreas awoke, the sun had not yet risen. It was obvious that Aurora was not yet awake. Boreas was trying to think of a way to sweep her off her feet, or even to just talk to her. Suddenly, he saw her walk outside and face World's End. As if it were the most natural thing in the world, the two began singing simultaneously, calling the dawn together. Melody and harmony mixed smoothly as the two sang. After seemingly an eternity, the sun rose, and both ended the song. Aurora looked at Boreas with love in her eyes, and he knew that this was only the start of their happiness. However, at that same moment, a chill wind caressed the two, causing both of them to shiver and make signs of warning against evil omens.

After many months the Olympians noticed that the sunrise was changing. The dawn seemed dimmer and paler, somehow even colder. After a few more months, the changes were much more pronounced. The dawn had definitely taken on a sickly greenish tint. Concerned, Jove summoned Aurora and Boreas to Mt. Olympus.

There was quite a commotion as Aurora entered the great hall. Aurora had also changed because she was the personification of the dawn. She looked wan, much thinner, and her skin had taken on a deathly pallor. Horrified, Luna and Sol rushed to her side. "Why, she's as cold as ice!" they exclaimed. "What have you done to her?" they demanded of Boreas.

"I haven't done anything to her!" Boreas said defensively. "I love her!"

"Boreas hasn't done anything to harm me," Aurora protested.

"But what else could have caused this condition?" Jove asked. "It is your very nature, Boreas. The dawn was never meant to be kept cold and secluded. Instead, the dawn should be warm and giving."

"I won't be parted from Boreas!" Aurora exclaimed.

"If you separate us, the sun will never rise again!"

"Now, Aurora," Juno scolded. "You can hardly go on much longer in your present condition. Jove and I propose that you visit Boreas only at night at his home in the North. During the day, you must stay at your home near World's End." Sadly, Aurora and Boreas left the great hall. They went their separate ways, promising each other to meet that night at Boreas's home in the North.

Aurora visited Boreas every evening at his home. Because they both loved calling the dawn together, they still sang the ancient song, even during the night when the sun couldn't come back to the Earth. So, rather than dawn, the northern lights, or northern dawn, came instead. And ever since that time we have had the northern lights, or aurora borealis, named after Aurora and Boreas, lovers who are as different as day and night.

ABOUT THE AUTHOR

Jamie Pflasterer lives in Tremont, Illinois, where he attends Tremont High School. His extracurricular activities include volleyball, speech, and the duties of secretary for his church's youth board. In his spare time, Jamie says, he enjoys "reading books and entertaining the family dog."

The leg bone's connected to the funny bone . . .

Patella (Alias the Kneecap)

by JOE HASLEY

I've never been an exceptional student, but there is one scientific term you can bet I'll never forget.

It was a cool day in the middle of May. The kind near the end of the school year that just drags on and on. Perhaps the most tedious thing about the last weeks of sixth grade was that I was so looking forward to junior high. I hated being treated like a kid all the time and being told where to sit at lunch and that I should keep my desk clean because, "It will lead to good habits in the future." Yes, the last days of sixth grade were tedious.

Except, of course, for the time that could easily be classified as The Greatest Day of My Career as a Student.

The time for science had arrived. Mr. Winnekamp asked, "Would anyone like to try the bone chart today?"

There was an “Oh yeah, right” and a “Dream on,” but all the snickering in the room turned to a dead hush when I said, “Yeah, Mr. Winnekamp. I’d like to take the challenge.”

Now, granted, in order to understand the magnitude of the moment, you may need some background. It had been announced the previous day that anyone who could name all twenty-six bones on the chart at the back of the room would receive twenty extra credit points and get their name on the “I Know My Bones” chart and would receive an official membership certificate to the “I Know My Bones” Club. But, as is always the case when such fame and glory are at stake, there was a catch: you only had one chance to take the membership test. One mistake, one wrong word, and your chance to be the best of the best went down the tubes in one fell swoop.

So now that you know the reason for the class’s amazement, I can continue where I left off.

Mr. Winnekamp and I walked to the back of the room with the class still reeling in shock. The only sound was that of my corduroy overalls as my legs swished together. It seemed like the longest walk of my life from my desk to the back of that room. When we finally arrived, the chart seemed like a giant peering down to seal my doom. The intensity was nerve-racking.

After an eternity, the solemn silence was broken by the sound of Mr. Winnekamp’s voice. “What is the name of this bone?” he asked, pointing to the head of the skeleton on the life-sized poster.

I looked around. Every eye was on me. For a brief second—and only a second, mind you—I might have felt a bit of nervousness run up and down my spine. But, being a Hasley of noble character, I straightened my back, looked him in the eye, and answered him.

"That's the cranium." The class let out a huge sigh of relief, but then became as mesmerized as it had been only seconds before when it realized that there were still twenty-five bones to go.

So on we went, me naming each bone he pointed to, in a process that seemed to take hours. After the first couple of bones, though, the class seemed to relax and feel confident I would answer them all correctly. Everyone was pulling for me and cheering every time I got one right. I felt like I was shooting free throws in the final game of the NCAA tournament. Finally we got to the last bone. It was the knee bone. The class, which seconds earlier had been buzzing with anticipation, now fell dead silent.

Now, usually I'm pretty cool under pressure. I've gotten up in front of large groups before and it's no big deal. But this, this was entirely different. Every eye was on me. Mouths hung open. No one breathed. Mr. Winnekamp even started to sweat. The temperature outside was a mild fifty degrees, but you could have fried an egg on my head. The air was so thick you could have hung a map in midair just by driving nails through it. (Well, maybe not that thick, but close!)

People were turning blue because they had forgotten to breathe, so I decided it was time to take some final, decisive action. Calmly, coolly, I started to answer—and then my mind went blank! I couldn't remember! Oh no! My chance for fame and glory shot down because I couldn't remember the scientific name for kneecap. Who needed to know this stuff, anyway?

I wanted desperately to just say "kneecap" and get it over with, but something inside me just wouldn't give up. I thought so hard I thought my head would explode. Then, at my lowest moment, when I was in the pit of despair, at the end of my rope, about to lose faith, it hit me. Like a ray of sunlight coming through to pierce the darkness of a torture chamber, it came.

I looked up. The class was hanging on my every breath. My throat was as dry as carpet. I straightened myself from my hunched position, grabbed hold of my overall straps, looked at the chart, and casually said, "Ah . . . I'm pretty sure that's the patella."

The whole room just exploded. Everyone was yelling and standing on their desks and patting me on the back and hugging me. I think I even saw some tears of joy wiped back. Mr. Winnekamp came up, shook my hand, and presented me with the award.

"It's possible that they may rename the school after you, ya know."

"Jeez, I don't know," I said, trying not to appear ungrateful. "Having the school named after me when I'm only twelve might interfere with my chances of having a 'normal' childhood."

Mr. Winnekamp said he understood.

There were three really good things that happened to me as a result of being the first in my class admitted to the "I Know My Bones" Club. First, I could wear my corduroy overalls to school and not have to worry about anyone picking me up by the straps and giving me a snuggy. Second, I had a lot of new friends. And third, I have missed a lot of questions on a lot of tests, but you can bet that I'll never be at a loss for an answer to the question, "What is the scientific name for the kneecap?"

ABOUT THE AUTHOR

Joe Hasley lives in Cedar Rapids, Iowa, and attends Linn-Mar Sr. High School in Marion. He enjoys biking, camping, hiking, and drama (he's played the lead role in six of the last eight school plays). His advice to other writers: "Your life, though it may seem average to you, is a new and exotic world to other people. Don't be afraid to write about your personal experiences."

Is a brother's love unconditional?

Death's Fortress

by *HASSAN LÓPEZ*

The two horses wearily made their way up the twisted, obscure path. Their bodies, lathered with sweat, heaved with effort and gleamed in the noonday sun. Their two riders were equally fatigued. Both were fair elves of legend; each was tall and thin, but well-muscled. Golden hair glistened and gray eyes shone from each. Their pointed, elfin ears were alert at every moment, searching for a sound of danger. But the only noises were the steady clip-clop of the horses' hooves on the rising broken path and the screeching of vultures and other scavengers flying above. The land around them was desolate and empty. Deep chasms unexpectedly appeared around them as the simple path led them between great cliffs of immense height. The smell of dust and dirt was in the air, and the riders' spirits were low.

Silverleaf turned to his older brother and frowned. They had been traveling for many days and nights but neither had spoken or complained, for they were on a mission, a quest for their people. For weeks they had been searching for an object, a gem of great beauty, the Earthstone. This precious jewel was the honored, holy relic of their people. Although they had never seen the gem, they worshipped it and for centuries had searched for it. Now they knew where it was. A being of incredible power and evil was holding it in his castle. This terrible creature was the Unholy One, the King of the Undead.

Undead were creatures of death and chaos that had once been mortals but had committed unthinkable sins and evils during their lifetimes. So when death came, they had not the pleasure of drifting as spirits throughout the planes in total bliss and beautiful peace. No, they had, in a sense, come back to life as undead to serve evil forever, to live in an eternal torment of pain and suffering equal to the sins they had committed. The elves' mission was to destroy the evil leader of the undead forces and return with the sacred Earthstone. It would not be easy.

When the pair finally reached the top of the hill, they looked with horrified eyes at the sight below. A fortress of evil loomed before them. Tall spires pierced the clouds, and dark windows peered at the dusty land. Atop the center pinnacle, a lone flag flew in the desert wind. It had no picture, no figure; it was just black. A sign of death it was, and it alone struck fear into the hearts of the two travelers. The elves in their splendid, golden armor looked down at this citadel of chaos, this castle of doom.

"Well, I'll be a wart on an orc! We've found it!"

The ugly thing hobbled down the corridor and quickly limped to a large door at the end of the hall. He quivered with fear before knocking on the door and then entering the sinful room. As soon as he entered, the creature scampered across the filthy floor and fell to his knees, his head bowed. Before him rose a sinister throne of ebony and obsidian. Sitting patiently upon this devilish throne was an indescribable horror.

This horrible creature looked down upon the pitiful, pathetic blob of quivering flesh with uncompassionate eyes—if you could call them eyes. They were more like two jewels of burning fire and frosty ice. One was deep scarlet red, the other albino, cold white. These eyes could strike fear into any living thing. The rest of the creature's body was just as fearsome. Chunks of rotting, maggot-infested flesh hung from the torso of the being. Bright white bones showed through in many places, and the rib cage of the thing was entirely visible. But most horrifying of all was the black, beating object within the ribs of the creature. A heart—a corrupted, evil heart—pumped within that evil form. It spewed forth lethal poison into every inch of the undead creature, but this had no effect on him. He was the Unholy One, the King of the Undead. And he was pleased. "Speak," he breathed in a spectral whisper of death.

"Master, two mortals approach the castle. They are *elves*, Master! They could be searching for the Foulrock. What shall we do, Master?"

"Yes, Charka, you are right. They *are* searching for the Earthstone, which you call the Foulrock. I have expected this to happen. They think themselves clever, but we know better, don't we, my faithful one?" The Unholy One laughed in a horrifying tone and Charka prostrated himself against the hard floor, fear pounding in his chest. This only amused the Undead King more. "Yes, Charka, we will greet them. They must have traveled long and hard. We must be hospitable . . ."

Silverleaf stared nervously at the giant castle walls before him and at the foul moat blocking their way. Tentacles appeared here and there in the contaminated, putrid water. Red eyes glowed from beneath the surface at the pair of elves, but all these obstacles posed no problem to the seasoned adventurers. It was the castle itself that stopped them. Those pitch-black impassable walls, the ghoulish towers of evil, the flag of doom and death: all combined to create the malignity of this midnight fortress. What cursed plague was contained within these mighty walls? "Only death awaits us there," Silverleaf mumbled to himself as he shuddered unconsciously.

"But what must be done *will* be done," his brother intoned, as he slowly raised his hands, fingers spread wide. Silverleaf imitated this gesture and slowly began chanting in unison with his brother. The elves stood still in perfect concentration for several seconds, and then their enchantment ended. They opened their silver eyes and smiled at each other with confidence as they turned to watch their mystical work unfold. The sinister drawbridge quietly and smoothly lowered until it became the needed bridge across the vile moat. A gaping hole of utter darkness confronted them, and they entered the place of death, praying that they would also leave.

The Unholy One's servant scurried down the passage. It whimpered suddenly at times when its flitting eyes caught a movement in the oppressive shadows. A goblin, the creature was characteristically timid and fearful. His short, fat, hairy form wobbled as he limped his way down the narrow hallway. His wide, frightened eyes darted from door to door and shadow to shadow along the wicked corridor. Finally, Charka found himself at the top of a twisting stairwell. He stared down through the darkness, gulped, and then slowly descended into the bowels of the Undead King's fortress. He whispered to himself so as to keep from running with fear from the hellish place. "Master says we are in no danger. Master says Charka need not be afraid. Master is very smart and wise. Yes, very wise to send Drarth after the stupid elves. The Drarth will take care of the mean, nasty elves. Master told Charka he must get Drarth." Charka suddenly squealed with terror. "Charka afraid of Drarth!"

Silverleaf followed close behind his brother. As he agilely made his way down the cobweb-covered corridor, he began to think of his beloved brother to get his mind off his evil surroundings. They had always been best friends (which is sometimes rare among brothers) and had loved and protected each other since birth. But one thing had always vexed him about his older brother. A thread of doubt had always been in his mind. His brother had always acted more like . . . well, a guardian. Yes, a guardian, instead of the loving brother that he should have been. The two had always been close, but something had been missing—that sacred bond between elf and elf, and especially between brother and brother. Sometimes it even seemed as if his brother treated him as a stranger, as a subordinate. "Bah," Silverleaf whispered. "That's nonsense. Concentrate on what you were sent to do and not on foolish notions that can distract you."

Suddenly, his brother stopped and Silverleaf walked up to see what he had spotted. It was a stairway down. "To the dungeon," Silverleaf's brother answered to his unspoken question. "The place where the foul King of the Undead most likely hid our blessed Earthstone!" Below them lay the most sinister, infernal place in the castle . . . a place where unspeakable tortures were performed . . . a place of death and decay. "We must go there now!" said Silverleaf's brother. But the younger elf disagreed.

"No, my brother. You are mistaken. The foul King would not be so foolish as to place such a powerful relic in anyone's care other than his own. And we know that his chambers are located in the higher, more powerful reaches of this evil castle. *That* is where we must go."

"Don't be a fool, Silverleaf. The dungeon of this fortress is surely the evilest, most dangerous area. Hundreds of guards are probably patrolling its dark depths at this very moment, protecting our holy Earthstone. And remember, I have been selected to lead this mission and you must listen to *me*. Now, follow me . . ."

Silverleaf stared at his brother with storming eyes as the thread in his mind tensed. Silverleaf watched him go to the top of the stairs and then gesture impatiently, signaling that the way was clear. Then he turned his back and began the descent; Silverleaf, shaking with fury, followed a step behind.

Charka stood before a gigantic door. The portal was marked with chaotic runes and sinister symbols. The goblin trembled with fear, finally summoned his minute amount of courage, and then took out an amulet. He carefully placed the magical charm into a small niche in the door that matched the shape of the relic. Immediately, Charka squeaked in terror and ran from the door with horror-driven speed. He did not stop running until he was in his cozy, simple quarters, under his straw bed. He knew what was in the dungeon cell that he had opened, and he did not want to be around when it left.

A whisper and a shadow escaped from that room. The door slowly creaked open and shut. The Drarth was loose.

They had searched for hours and still not found anything. Silverleaf frowned with frustration. *I should not be upset. This dungeon is a labyrinth of rooms and corridors. There must be many more rooms that we have not seen and explored. It will be a while before our search is complete*, he thought. But deep inside, he was very worried. They had not found the Earthstone—that was no surprise—but neither had they found anything else: no monsters or minions of the Unholy One, no traps set to discourage unwelcome "visitors," nothing! They had expected the place to be crawling with demons and devils, and they had been prepared to deal with that. But there was nothing. It was as if everyone and everything had deserted the place, had just left. Something was wrong. Suddenly, Silverleaf's brother motioned for him to stop. Silverleaf looked ahead and saw that the corridor opened into a gigantic chamber. The two slowly entered. Their elfin eyes scanned the room, but it was empty. Another disappointment. They slowly began to cross the spidery room to the opposite side where the corridor continued. But just as they reached the center of the huge chamber, two glowing portcullises fell, blocking both entrance and exit. The magical iron bars of the gates had sealed them to their fate in the room. They were trapped.

"You released the Drarth?"

"Yes, Master. I did just as you wished."

"Excellent. Now we wait. And enjoy."

"Foul luck! Just as we suspected—they are magically protected, so we cannot open them with spells!" Silverleaf cursed with a note of panic in his voice.

"Calm down, Silverleaf. This is truly bad luck but it's certainly not the end of our quest. I don't know how I could have missed that trap. It was so obvious. And *you* were especially trained to see such things! By

Ferox's beard—think, man, think!"

Silverleaf felt the thread in his mind strain even more as his anger at his brother increased. But soon he calmed himself and dismissed his older brother's insult. *Now do what he said, Silverleaf. Think . . .*

Suddenly, the room was still. It was as if the very air was frozen. Then they heard a silent whisper of wind entering the room as an unseen shadow slipped noiselessly through the magical bars. The elves immediately felt a tremendous evil in the chamber. Something was there with them—and it was deadly. The two drew their slender swords, and the sound of metal scraping on metal broke the strange silence. Desperately, they searched the room for a sign of what was with them. It settled and then it grew. It took shape and form before the elves' terrified eyes. It was pure evil.

The thing grew into a twisted mass of darkness. Two heavily muscled arms and legs took shape. A body of incredible size connected them, and the demonic head formed. Bat-like wings sprouted from the creature's massive back. Horns, fangs, and claws appeared. Two red eyes of intense evil stared at the petrified elves. A colossus of death towered over them. It was a Drarth, an undead creature of immense power and a favorite of the Unholy One. It had come to kill, and its victims were before it!

Silverleaf began to tremble as the terror within him rose. He felt his soul being squeezed out of him. *Get a hold of yourself*, thought Silverleaf. *Calm down or perish!*

He regained his composure, and he and his brother began to react swiftly and calmly. They knew that they alone could not handle this thing. They immediately began chanting and slowly gesturing, weaving a spell that would, with luck, save their precious lives. Their training proved worthy; they finished before the Drarth could move one heavy muscle. Instantly, another creature appeared before them. The elves had summoned an Olgrod, a being of destruction and doom. It had the body of an enormous horse with two tentacles flailing on each flank, the head of an old woman crying tears of pain and sorrow, and the tail of a salamander. It screeched a cry of anguish and reared up before the evil Drarth. It too had been called to kill. It was prepared to fulfill its mission.

The two beings of power immediately locked in a desperate battle for survival. Tentacles whipped, fangs snapped, and claws scraped. The two were an even match; the elves cringed as they watched the balance tip from one to the other. Then the Drarth opened its gaping mouth, and a torrent of acid poured forth onto the Olgrod. The summoned creature reared back in pain as the burning, bubbling substance ate away at its face. Tears of acid dripped from the bleeding eyes.

The Drarth saw its advantage. It leapt forth, ready to finish the kill. But the Olgrod was not totally stunned. It whipped up its four tentacles and plucked the Drarth right from the air. Two bolts of lightning suddenly shot from the Olgrod's blinded eyes and entered the Drarth's squirming form. The undead monster mouthed a silent scream as electricity flowed through its pain-racked body. Finally, it fell limp and, ever so slowly, began to fade into nothingness. In seconds, it disappeared, and with it its killer. The Olgrod's task was completed. It was needed no more.

Silverleaf stared into the astonished eyes of his

brother. Both knew that they would never again see anything as incredible as what they had just witnessed.

The Unholy One sat still, deep in thought, on his throne of darkness. "This was unexpected. It is most unfortunate, but not disastrous. These elves are more powerful than I had expected. I could use this power." The King of the Undead smiled then. "Yes, I know what I will do. They may enjoy victory for the moment, but soon they will be surprised. Very surprised . . ."

Silverleaf and his companion stood before a door. Minutes after the battle between the Drarth and the Olgrod had finished, while they were searching for a way out of their prison, they had been teleported to a long hallway. This blood-red door was at the end of that corridor. Both knew that the Undead King had teleported them there. *They had been summoned by the Unholy One to confront him!* And Silverleaf was afraid. They had barely managed to survive this long, and the hardest part of their quest was yet to come. Would they come out of it alive? Silverleaf looked at his brother and saw only confidence written on his face. This reassured him and, at the same time, pricked his resentment of his brother even more. Silverleaf then felt his brother's hand come into his own. The two opened the bleeding door to reveal the evilest chamber in the realm . . .

An odor of decaying flesh assailed their nostrils and caused them to gag in sickness. Lines of undead terrors stood obscenely before them: skeletons, shadows, wights, wraiths, specters, spooks, ghouls and ghosts, zombies, demons, and devils all stood together as one. The putrid vestiges of evil had horrible grins chiseled on their decrepit faces, their rotting flesh, black, poisoned blood, and white, skeletal bones making the elves freeze with terror. Behind this phalanx of death was a deep chasm filled with boiling, acidic lava in which could be seen floating various body parts.

The Unholy One, the leader of this ghastly army, stood with glowing eyes staring at his horrified guests. "I see you have come to visit me, foolish mortals. In doing so, you have also come to visit death! Attack, sweet children! Kill them!"

Slowly, the horde of undead lumbered toward the pair. But to Silverleaf, they were marching toward him alone! His sanity was slipping away, the terror of what was before him causing him to lose all sense of reality. The quest had begun to take its toll. They were after him and him alone. They were going to torture his soul in the foul kingdom of the undead. His eyes became hysterical, and he dropped his sword to the stone floor. "Stop!" he cried. "Please! Don't hurt me!"

He flailed his arms in front of him as if to ward off the invaders who were slowly advancing. But they kept coming. They would not stop.

Suddenly he knew what would make them stop! At that moment, all the doubts and thoughts that had collected in his mind about his brother exploded and destroyed the rest of his sensibility. The thread tensed and then, finally, snapped. He turned to his older brother and grabbed his arm in an iron grip. He stared into his brother's equally horrified eyes. These eyes told the whole story. They knew what Silverleaf was thinking and they pleaded with him: *No! I love you. I have always tried to protect you because I cared for you. Please!*

But Silverleaf did not hear. To him, this was not his brother and never had been. To him, it was his only way out of this terrible place. He was not Silverleaf anymore. He pushed his brother with all his might into the swarm of death. The seething mass of undead clawed and ripped at the elf. Blood flew as screams of terror and pain erupted into the air. The mass of undead then slowly made its way back toward the chasm, dragging Silverleaf's brother behind them. One by one, the dead fell into the fiery magma and then the elf toppled in. Every creature soon disappeared beneath the deadly liquid, and the room was suddenly empty. Except for two: Silverleaf and the Unholy One.

The King of the Undead laughed. It was then that Silverleaf realized what he had just done. He fell to the floor, weeping. "What have I done? What have I done?" he cried.

"What have you done?" the Unholy One whispered. "You have sealed your fate, that's all! You have just committed a costly sin, my child. Yes, you murdered your own brother—just to save your own worthless life."

The Undead King laughed again knowingly. "You do know what that means, don't you? Here, let me explain, my child: you are now mine. You have just done a totally foul, evil thing. You must be punished for that." Silverleaf's eyes grew wide with horror. "Yes, I see that you understand, my child," the Unholy One said with a cruel smile. "You have become your own enemy—that which you journeyed here to kill. You will forever be tortured for the sin you have just committed. Death will never be truly yours. For when you die, you will not be free. You will be mine."

Silverleaf felt complete and total despair in his soul. He knew that the Undead King spoke the truth. One day, he would suffer for his evil act. He slowly picked himself up and headed for the exit of the castle. There was no spirit left in Silverleaf to continue the quest. He was a loner now and forever would be. As he was crossing the drawbridge of the evil fortress, he turned back and looked up at the flag of death waving in the wind. And he heard a voice whisper in his ear:

"Godspeed! I await your return, my child . . ."

ABOUT THE AUTHOR

Hassan López lives in Nichols, New York, and attends Tioga Central High School in Tioga Center. He reports: "I enjoy staring at the stars, and my favorite hobby is writing fantasy and short stories." Hassan has authored a fantasy board game currently being considered for publication.

My life as a closet chess master . . .

The Mudders

by Rachel Leverenz

If Mama knew I played chess with the Mudder brothers, I don't figure I'd have much of the skin on my behind left. See, with Mama you had to be real careful, 'cause even though she wore Mary Kay lipstick and a French twist in her hair, she had an awful quick eye and was sure to catch any behind that was fixing to be out of hand. And Mama was as sneaky as the water snake I caught with my fishing pole on the Copper River, and, between me and Mr. Newman, who happened to be on the same bank at the same time, I took that water snake home and hid her in my socks and underwear drawer for a week straight and named her Ramona after my mama, until Mama herself began to notice that my socks smelled funny, and Ramona found Ramona in my socks and underwear drawer quick as the blink of your eye.

See, the Mudder brothers lived in town across from the bingo hall where Mrs. Mudder played every Saturday night, twenty-three cards at a time. It's no wonder Mrs. Mudder won the jackpot every weekend, as she held bingo jamborees in her basement when Mr. Mudder went out to the Soda & Suds Bar which, to be straight, was more or less every evening. And so Mrs. Mudder got her practicing done through the night until Mr. Mudder came home, drunk silly and mad, and he would stampede all Mrs. Mudder's practice mates out the door in a hurry.

See, the Mudder brothers were named after Mrs. Mudder's favorite roasted wiener on a campfire night and Mr. Mudder's favorite childhood cartoon dog, and so, sad as it was, the Mudder brothers were named Oscar and Snoopy. Mama called the whole family crazy termites and low as the roots of a dogwood tree, and if I was ever caught playing with them, she would tear my eyeballs out and feed them to my dog, Frisco, and bury me in the sewer and let the flies eat me for supper. And Mama said she would then up and move to South America where no one would know her only son had been germed by a sleazy family with a bingo nut wife, a drunken husband, and a wiener and a dog for sons, and that I'd best behave 'cause she, by golly, didn't want to live in South America.

All the same, dangerous as it was, I liked the Mudders and I figure they liked me too, because Mrs. Mudder would fix me cheese and mustard sandwiches with cold cappuccino when I came to play chess with the Mudder brothers. We played in Mrs. Mudder's bedroom closet, with a Coleman lantern dangling from a clothes hanger above us, and with Mrs. Mudder's beady skirts and blouses that smelled like monkey urine getting stuck in our hair, and her high heel shoes with the alligator heads at the tip stabbing our knees, and our cheese and mustard sandwiches smeared all over the chessboard, and the mothballs making us sneeze and cough, and all the while playing rounds and rounds of chess.

See, Oscar was two years older than Snoopy, but no smarter. His feet were too big, and he had awful buckteeth, and Mama said he was fit to be in a cage. One time Oscar was in line to see a movie at the picture show, and a younger girl in front of him turned around and saw Oscar with his finger plunged into his nose. She wrinkled her own nose and said disgustedly, "Pardon me, sir, but you are picking your nose!"

Oscar only grinned real silly and replied, "Naw! I'm just pointing to my brain!" Some people wonder if he's even got one. I know Mama's not too sure.

Snoopy, on the other hand, most surely did have a brain, seeing as how he won the county spelling bee in 1952. Mama said Snoopy was the lucky one of the bunch, more or less like the only raisin in a bowl of stale wheat flakes.

I don't guess Mama ever questioned my going to the movies in town so often other than the suspicion of a girl, which threw me off completely and struck me silly at the thought. No, it wasn't any silly girl in a flowered dress and bobbed hair; it was just the plain old Mudders and a couple of rounds of chess in Mrs. Mudder's bedroom closet.

I was right successful in my sneaking to the Mudders' for two years straight, and awful proud of the slyness that I had no doubt picked up from my own mama's genes, and sometimes I was even a mite swollen-headed . . . all until that silly afternoon when all my dreads turned to reality, and I thought maybe I would be fed to the sewer flies after all.

See, Mama didn't fancy me going to town in my shorts and T-shirts, and so she dressed me all proper in navy blue slacks and a collared striped shirt. Then she inspected me closely, a Camel dangling from her ruby lips, her head cocked to one side and all dolled up in a fancy French twist, her long, slender fingers smoothing the wrinkles on the front of my shirt before she scooted me out the door, calling, "Don't stain your socks!" I don't think Mama ever played chess.

And so it was, as I crossed the street from the bingo hall, all proper and looking nice, my hair slicked back, my collar ironed and buttoned, my socks nice and white. Somehow, though, just as I hit the first step of the Mudders' front porch, my shirt came untucked, my slacks wrinkled, my hair slipped over my eyes and ears, and then I entered the Mudders'.

I can't figure how Mama got the notion to visit Aunt Tommie Sue on that awful day in June; they hadn't talked for years after Mama stole Aunt Tommie's Avalon perfume, which promised on the front label that all the movie stars wore it, sure as sugar. Aunt Tommie Sue bought it right out of a shop in Hollywood where Uncle Hank ran the motion pictures.

Aunt Tommie Sue lived two blocks from the Mudders on Thirty-third Street, beside the Betty Jo Barber Shop where she got her hair done every week in bobs and curls, which she claimed looked just like the movie stars'. And Aunt Tommie Sue lived in a bright pink house that looked right suitable for Strawberry Shortcake, and she wore mink fur coats, smoked Camels, and wore purple lipstick, just like the movie stars.

The trouble was that Mama had to walk right on past the Mudders' house to get to Aunt Tommie Sue's pink house on Thirty-third Street. It all wouldn't have happened if it hadn't been so sticky hot that day; the thought of playing chess all cramped in Mrs. Mudder's closet with the smell of monkey urine tingling in our noses didn't much appeal to Oscar, Snoopy, or me, and so we settled on the front porch with our cheese and mustard sandwiches to play a few rounds of chess.

See, Mr. Mudder decided on coming home early that day from the Soda & Suds, nonetheless drunk and mad, and Mrs. Mudder's bingo jamboree in the basement was loud and wild as ever, and I don't figure who timed it so perfect, whether it was Mama and her Camels, Mr. Mudder, or Mrs. Mudder and her jamboree mates. All the same, just as Mama turned the corner and caught a glimpse of the Mudders' front porch and Oscar and his buckteeth, Snoopy and his cheese sandwich, and me right between them, she let out one of her awful screams, the Camel falling from her mouth. At the same moment, Mr. Mudder started cussing, and a whole stampede of bingo women came pouring out of the house, knocking over our chessboard, Mrs. Mudder trotting along behind them. Then everybody grew quiet, and Mrs. Mudder flashed her silly grin and asked, "Anyone for another sandwich?"

I don't recall much after that except the awful pain in my ear as Mama dragged me off the Mudders' porch and I watched Oscar and Snoopy staring, dumbfounded, at me and Mama. I couldn't help thinking, "I hope them flies aren't hungry."

ABOUT THE AUTHOR

Rachel Leverenz attends Northern High School in her hometown of Accident, Maryland. A self-described leader who "loves to help," she was last year's president of Northern Middle School and is presently a team member in soccer, softball, downhill skiing, and Little League baseball. She has been writing stories "since I was old enough to pick up a pencil," and has written several longer pieces. Being close to nature and spending time with her family are special joys.

Only *she* knew the secret of the dragon . . .

Parade of Dragons

by Nicole Ball

The sun coursed its way through the heavens. From its high perch in the sky, it looked down upon the earth, a silent and solitary observer of men's lives and actions. As its golden rays began to warm far-off China, it spied a figure not unlike itself in silence and solitude. The figure sat quiet and alone, a short distance from an active hive of scurrying people.

The figure was motionless, seemingly entranced by the activity before it. The wind rustled its red silk shirt, so bright that it seemed to burn like liquid fire. The yellow cuffs and collar on the shirt, reflecting the sun's blinding rays, dazzled the eye as molten gold. Rivaling the very sapphire depths of the nearby ocean, blue silk pants floated above black shoes, which were delicate in appearance but sturdy in nature.

The figure's hair was black as the dark veil of midnight and cropped short and simply. A casual observer might have mistaken the figure for a boy, in fact, so short was the hair and so masculine the attire. But a more attentive observer would have noticed that the figure was somewhat small and possessed of a strange grace and delicacy. This, as well as the flowing curves of the face and the delicately chiseled features, not lacking in beauty, gave away the fact that the pretty Mai-Ling was a girl.

She sat, eyes sparkling with excitement and a peculiar longing, watching the group before her. It consisted of a vast swarm of active boys, gathered from several surrounding villages. She watched her older brother, Hikaru, working hard in their midst.

Many of the older boys were applying the final touches to the dozens of unfinished wooden and metal frames which were scattered about the area, looking like oddly shaped wire cages. The other boys were divided between covering the finished frames with brightly colored silk, carrying frames in and out of a large storage building, and assembling what appeared to be huge masks for the frames. Hikaru was busily attaching levers and pulleys, many of which were linked to bottles that contained colored liquids, to the inside of the most enormous frame, which was very high and long, and half-covered with billowing green silk.

As Mai-Ling observed the work, she tried to imagine what the many frameworks would look like when they were completed. Her mind turned back to the parade of the previous year. She had thought then, as she watched the magnificent costumes and floats, as well as the enormous dragon, that they could not be improved upon. And yet, this year's parade, supposedly, would far surpass anything the people had seen for at least half a century.

The highlight of the entire parade would be the framework that Hikaru was working on. It was to be a mammoth dragon and would lead most of the parade. Her brother, considered by many people to be extraordinarily intelligent, was attaching special equipment to the dragon so that, when inside, he would be able to make the dragon breathe fire and smoke and accomplish other exciting feats. The equipment was very complicated and he, who had designed it all, was the only one of the many boys and men who understood it well enough to operate it. Mai-Ling was very proud that she, too, knew how to work it, having been taught by Hikaru for several weeks at home. But that was a secret known only between brother and sister. She sighed. If only she could help with the parade! It had been her most sacred dream, ever. When she was five, she had learned that girls were banned from participating in preparations for the great parade.

As Mai-Ling continued to watch, several of the younger boys, whose sole job was to fetch and carry for the older ones, ran aside to a dozen large boxes, which were very near to Mai-Ling. She knew that they contained more silk and material for the covering of the frameworks. The small boys struggled with the heavy cords which bound the large boxes. One particularly small boy, only about five or six, worked feverishly but to no avail. The ropes did not loosen, and the other boys ignored the child's efforts. Mai-Ling glanced at her own long, slender hands and knew it would take but a moment for her nimble fingers to undo the ropes. Surely no one would mind her doing that small task. It certainly wouldn't hurt anything.

Nevertheless, she glanced around and waited until no one was watching before she ventured toward the small boy. He sank gratefully to his knees as her fingers flew across the knotted ropes, loosening them. Mai-Ling worked quickly and silently. The longer it took, the faster her heart beat. What if one of the older boys saw her helping? Hikaru had fought with all his influence to convince the other boys, and the older men who oversaw the parade preparations, to allow Mai-Ling to watch. It had not been easy. If she were caught, even he might not be able to convince them to allow her to continue to watch.

But, within a moment, Mai-Ling's thoughts had changed from fear to hot anger and indignation. Surely no one would care if she untied ropes! It was such a menial task. Yet she accepted it as if it were a great blessing. It was ridiculous that they should refuse to allow girls to participate, and they certainly shouldn't mind what she was doing. And yet, if they did—

Her thoughts were cut short by a steel-like grip descending upon her shoulder. She felt a hand pull her back roughly and unexpectedly. Mai-Ling stumbled backwards and, losing her balance, fell sprawling into the dirt.

Above her towered a boy of seventeen or so, his face contorted with anger. He shouted at her, condemning her actions as though they were terrible crimes. His angry accusations began to draw a crowd, to Mai-Ling's utter dismay. In a moment, one of the men who oversaw the parade preparations was coming slowly across the grounds, leaning heavily on his thick, carved staff.

Upon his arrival the boy's shouts subsided, but a

dark look of fury rested on his brow as he explained to the old man, in short and violently angry bursts of words, what he had seen Mai-Ling doing. The old man listened silently and, when the boy was finally quiet, turned and regarded Mai-Ling with a somewhat quizzical look in his eyes.

She squirmed under the intense gaze. To her, the seconds, as his expressionless eyes probed her face, seemed like years, and so she had aged a century before he finally spoke.

"Take her home, Hikaru," the old man said quietly. "She will not return until she has learned her place."

Hikaru, who Mai-Ling discovered at her side, bowed slightly in compliance and led Mai-Ling, her cheeks flaming with anger and embarrassment, from the slowly thinning group.

The walk home for Mai-Ling seemed the most frustrating one she had ever taken in her life. Her brother listened silently as her scorching thoughts attempted to transform into words that would express her outrage, and he comforted her with gentle words when the outburst was over and the tears came.

The next few weeks passed slowly for Mai-Ling. She moved about restlessly throughout the day and often dreamed of how the work on the parade was progressing. Her moods swiftly changed from anger over the unfairness of everything, to embarrassment over the memory of the eyes of the scornful boys, to depressed silence at the thought that she had spoiled her opportunity to watch the parade preparations, and to jealousy directed at the boys who could participate, while she was banned.

Her sympathetic parents, who had always encouraged her tendencies no matter how strange they often seemed for a young girl, said nothing of the matter after Hikaru had taken them aside and explained quietly what had happened. They did not even mention the parade, after discovering that the thought of it was nearly unbearable to Mai-Ling. Even Hikaru avoided the subject, although he and Mai-Ling had shared many previous conversations about the parade and his exciting controls for the great dragon.

As the days crawled by and the parade day neared, people from the surrounding villages flooded the nearby city. They filled every available space, and many were forced to sleep outside. Guards were posted each night by the floats to ensure that no curious visitors would disturb them.

The day before the parade, after Hikaru had finished working, he and Mai-Ling took a dragon kite which they had made together several months before and went to fly it in a more open space on the outskirts of the village. In this way, Hikaru distracted Mai-Ling's longing and interrupted her sorrowful gazes toward the place where the last touches were being put on the parade.

Mai-Ling's mind forgot for a time the unsettling events that had seized her emotions for so many days. How the kite soared and swooped! Climbing on the currents of the wind, it looked like a dragon out of a magical legend come alive.

And then, as the wind will do at the most inopportune moments, it stopped. The dragon kite, at the end of its long string, hovered a moment and then dropped, straight and hard as a stone, despite the frantic pulls by Mai-Ling. With a crash, it hit the roof of a nearby house.

Tears glistened in Mai-Ling's eyes as she speculated on the possible damage to the wonderful creation. Surely dragons must be a curse to her! Dragons were in the parade from which she had been banned, and the most-likely ruined kite was a dragon, too.

As her mind filled with these thoughts, Hikaru ruffled her hair, gave her arm a quick squeeze, and dashed away toward the house. Mai-Ling watched him talking with a woman at the door. After a moment's conversation, he disappeared behind the house. When he returned, he was carrying a ladder, which he promptly set against a wall. He climbed nimbly up, walked across the roof, retrieved the kite, and waved to Mai-Ling.

It was then that the catastrophe came. As Hikaru turned and waved, his foot slipped, and, in a moment, he lost his balance and fell. Mai-Ling screamed as he hit the ground with a dull thud, his left leg twisted beneath him.

Her terrified screams immediately drew a small crowd. The woman from the house, several of her neighbors, and three men who were walking along the street came rushing, but Mai-Ling was there first.

For the rest of her life, Mai-Ling could never clearly recall what happened in those next few minutes. She vaguely remembered one of the women comforting her, trying to ease her hysterical sobbing, as the men carefully carried Hikaru home.

The doctor was sent for, and he quickly came. He found Hikaru lying on a couch, pale from pain and occasionally groaning. Mai-Ling waited on the outside steps while the doctor treated her brother's injuries. She could not bear the sight of his white face. Afterwards, however, she returned and, quietly sobbing as she knelt by Hikaru's head, listened as the doctor made his diagnosis.

"His left leg is broken," he said quietly to Mai-Ling's mother, his fingertips brushing the splint on Hikaru's leg. "His right arm was twisted badly and will be useless for at least a week. I've treated the blow to his head. That will be fine. But," the doctor added, turning to look Hikaru straight in the eyes, "it will be impossible for you to participate in the parade."

Hikaru groaned softly. "But I'm the only one who knows how to work the dragon's head! I was to operate it during the parade. It was going to be the highlight of the whole parade, and there's no time to teach anyone, even if I were well enough to. The parade will be a failure without it!" He broke off bitterly, angry at himself for not being more careful. Just then his anguished eyes caught a glimpse of Mai-Ling, who, oblivious to his comments, was watching him with a tear-stained face.

"Mai-Ling," he said quietly, a faint light of hope growing in his eyes, "go to the parade grounds. Tell one of the boys what has happened and ask him to tell Tsing Tao that I need to speak to him immediately."

Mai-Ling nodded and ran off, as fast as the wind itself. She had no idea who Tsing Tao was, and so, when the boy she had spoken with introduced her to the old man who was the overseer of the entire parade, she was shocked.

She guided the old man to their house and waited outside while he and Hikaru talked. Presently, her mother emerged and sank gracefully to the ground beside Mai-Ling. Her arms enveloped Mai-Ling and she comforted her wordlessly, as only mothers can do for their children.

There was a murmur of voices inside the house, and, after a short time, Tsing Tao emerged. He looked at Mai-Ling and said quietly, "Come. Walk with me." Astonished but obedient, Mai-Ling followed in silence.

The silence continued as the pair walked slowly away from the house and the quiet bustle of the village. Tsing Tao seemed to be reflecting on some difficulty. It could only be the fact that he would have no dragon for the parade, Mai-Ling thought despairingly.

Finally, the old man stopped and turned to regard Mai-Ling impassively. Abruptly he spoke. "Your brother tells me you know how to operate the dragon's head."

Mai-Ling gulped and murmured a barely audible "Yes" as she nodded her head.

The man continued. "If you can prove to me that you can make the dragon breathe fire and smoke, if you can make its eyes glow red, if you can make the head turn and the mouth open, then you, Mai-Ling, shall do so tomorrow."

Mai-Ling was astounded. Her eyes widened and a wave of overwhelming joy made her tremble. Tears of utter amazement flooded her eyes, and her mouth quavered between a smile, a laugh, and a shout. Hardly able to speak for excitement, she tried to control her feelings. Gulping desperately, she said quietly, "I can do these things that you ask, and I will prove it to you now, if you wish, with actions, not words." Tsing Tao inclined his head slightly in a faint nod and led the way to the dragon.

Mai-Ling had no memory of the journey back to the village. Her feet wanted to run, but she held them back for the slow steps of Tsing Tao. After an eternity, they returned to the grounds from which Mai-Ling had been banished a short time before.

Her hands trembled and her heart nearly choked her as, to the amazement of all the boys, she slipped inside the dragon and took her place at the controls. Her shaking hands quickly acquainted themselves with the controls that she had not seen since they were installed in the dragon. Steadying herself, she began.

The levers and gears responded instantly to her commands. Her swift fingers swept over a pulley, and the dragon's mouth opened. Flames poured forth. Another motion and smoke billowed from the dragon's nostrils. A menacing glow gleamed in the red eyes in response to another move. When she had finished everything that she could think of to do, she ended the performance and emerged from the dragon head. Only then was she aware that *all* the boys, young and old, had stopped their work to gather in a crowd around the dragon.

Mai-Ling approached Tsing Tao and looked for approval in his eyes. He spoke quietly. "You have made the dragon come alive. You shall do so again tomorrow." He made a formal bow and, turning away, hobbled off.

There was complete silence. Then, as Mai-Ling moved to leave, the crowd, consisting of dozens of boys, moved apart and formed two straight lines. Mai-Ling was at the head of the path between the lines. Understanding their intentions, she walked slowly down the path. Her heart thrilled as she saw the boys that she passed, bowing respectfully to her. At the end of one of the lines, Mai-Ling recognized the boy who had pulled her to the ground. He did not speak, but his bow, lower and more respectful than any of the others, asked forgiveness. Mai-Ling gave it to him in a gentle smile, which he could not help but understand.

The next day Mai-Ling was up early. She dressed in her blue, red, and yellow silk attire and slipped on her black shoes. She danced about the house, excited, counting the minutes until the time came for her to go and take her place inside the great dragon.

Hikaru ruffled her hair and wished her good luck. He would be taken to the city later in a cart, so that he could watch the festivities. Her mother embraced her with tears in her eyes, and her father gave her an encouraging smile and a gentle squeeze on her shoulder. Once out of the house, Mai-Ling ran, filled with a giddy feeling as though she were flying.

It did not take long for her to make her way through the gathering crowds to the great dragon's head. There were a dozen girls in beautiful dresses who would head the parade, doing a traditional dance along the way. Behind them, young girls would follow, throwing confetti and brightly colored streamers. The rest of the parade consisted of the many boys who would work the floats and dragons. Mai-Ling was the only girl among them.

Finally, the time came for the parade to begin. Mai-Ling took her place inside the dragon and looked out of small holes made for her to see through. She watched the dancers take their places, and she heard the music begin. The dancers and the girls with confetti began to move forward. Musicians followed. Then, nearly a dozen small dragons, without any special effects, followed the musicians, weaving in and out, across the street, in a lively dance.

And then—it was time! Mai-Ling took her first thrilling step forward. Her heart beat quickly with nervousness as she began to move slowly. Her hands trembled with excitement. She watched as all eyes turned to her dragon as it began to move down the street, carried by over a dozen boys, with her at the head by the controls.

Shouts, claps, and cheers erupted from the crowd. Mai-Ling's hands flew, and again the dragon came alive, as if by magic. The great head turned and the eyes glowed with hot fury. Smoke billowed and flames crackled as the giant beast moved forward. It was alive—more alive than it had ever been before!

The crowds gasped at the reality of it all, and small children hid their faces in fear, while others crowed with delight. Mai-Ling's heart leaped with joy as she passed Hikaru and her parents, broad smiles on all their faces.

The smoke from the dragon billowed upward, higher and higher, until it reached the sun. The sun gazed down on the parade below, one of the greatest China had ever seen. That day, the sun saw many happy and proud young girls, but surely, nowhere in all of China, or, quite possibly, the world, was there one so absolutely happy and so very, very proud.

ABOUT THE AUTHOR

Nicole Ball wrote this story at Frontier Central High School in her hometown of Hamburg, New York. A longtime Trekkie, Nicole collects Star Trek memorabilia. She also maintains a large doll collec-

tion, many of which are porcelain and dressed in the traditional garments of their respective countries. Nicole's Chinese doll provided inspiration for the main character in this story. Other favorite pastimes include reading (sci-fi, fantasy, mystery, and classics) and writing. "Parade of Dragons" won the 1995/96 Paul A. Witty Short Story Award, presented by the International Reading Association.

Story Index

By genre, topic, and for use as writing models

By Genre

By Topic